Tigers in the Wood

ILLINOIS SHORT FICTION

A list of books in the series appears at the end of this volume.

Rebecca Kavaler

Tigers in the Wood

UNIVERSITY OF ILLINOIS PRESS

Urbana and Chicago

*Publication of this work was supported in part by a grant
from the Illinois Arts Council, a state agency.*

*Some of these stories were written and this book
organized with the help of a fellowship from
the National Endowment for the Arts.*

This book is printed on acid-free paper.

"Tigers in the Wood," *Yale Review,* Winter, 1981.
"The Zeigarnik Effect," *Mid-American Review,* Fall, 1981.
"Those Grand Old Songs," *Yale Review,* Spring, 1983.
"Little Boy Blue," *Carolina Quarterly,* Spring-Summer, 1980.

Library of Congress Cataloging-in-Publication Data

Kavaler, Rebecca.
  Tigers in the wood.

  Contents: Tigers in the wood—Depression glass—Local habitations—[etc.]
  (Illinois short fiction)
  I. Title.   II. Series.
PS3561.A8685T5   1986   813'.54   85-24648
ISBN 0-252-01308-5 (alk. paper)

Contents

Tigers in the Wood

Something was about to happen, the weather proclaimed. The air was expansive. The trees threw off a grey-green haze, a smokiness, a smoldering.

"Not here." Even the dog sniffed spring. She tightened up on the leash. "Down below in the park you'll have a run."

Everything can be borne but a succession of beautiful days. A purely seasonal urge, she forgave herself, this scrawling how true! on the blank margins of someone else's thought.

"Professor." The campus security guard saluted her with his stick. Police—last of mankind to saunter. He stood on the corner with her while she waited for the light to change. He wished it would make up its mind, he complained of the weather. Across the street, California, squeezed between Vermont and Illinois, struggled to unpark. He eyed the wheel-turning judiciously.

"Some guy jumped out of a fifteen floor window this morning—from that building there in the next block. See the tarp on the sidewalk? Never knew a woman to jump—you ever notice that? Always a man, seems like."

"I'm sorry to hear it," she said.

The light turned. He shook his head reprovingly at a screeching of brakes.

"Take care, Professor," he said easily and headed back up the hill to the campus.

Red light.

Foot shifted instinctively to brake, but he had no intention of stopping. Luck was with him, his foot still on the ready when the sharply angled car jerked into the roadway from a too-tight parking space. The brakes screamed but he held himself aloof, leaving his hand to make its own obscene retort. The vacated parking space became his destination, decided upon and reached instantaneously. Like being God.

The engine stopped. Godhood spluttered and died away. The sensation of speed, of his body maintaining its forward jetlike propulsion, lasted longer. Somewhere in the back of his skull a red beacon of light began to revolve again, flashing on, off, on, off. He re-walked the long block from the corner grocery, reabsorbed the shock of the parked patrol car. As if in a problem-solving dream, he reworked the scene: walked coolly up the stoop, swinging the six-pack he had gone out for, past the out-of-order elevator, up the stinking stairs, walked in on cops for company. Surprise, surprise. And after the surprise, convincingly registered, remembered his manners. Can I offer you? Unzipped a can with the careless air of a man ready to sit down to TV. A working man (but maybe Edie had already told them he was fired?). The wife don't keep me stocked, you see. A working man, unvalued in his home. A bit of plaintiveness to undermine her I-always-knew-it'd-come-to-this smirk.

Sure, that's the way he should have played it. Would have, too, but for the red light on top of the cop car. In one quarter-turn, it had blinked out the man, blinked back the boy. He was the kid ducking in a doorway with all the sweaty guilt of teenage truancy, knowing he was home too early but feeling sick from the fried meat pie snitched from a street vendor, seeing a cop (Pop? no, not Pop) amble down the steps. The flash of a grin, the pluck at the crotch, a V-for-victory sign wagged at the partner waiting in the car, and they were gone. Up the stairs, soft-footed step, the slightest jar inciting the stomach to roil, letting himself in as stealthily as if he were picking the lock, hoping not to be seen. Not being seen. Seeing instead. Through the open bedroom door, his mother's naked thighs, spread apart, obscene V, sticky with slimy aftermath. Beaver, beaver, cleft with a cleaver. Belly pierced with a griping pain.

A fool to cut and run. He lifted his clenched hands from the wheel, surprised not to leave the skin of his palms behind. The hands made a jerky movement of disgust and fell back on the wheel, but limply, washing themselves of such a fool. He should have stayed. He knew how to handle cops. He had a special smile for cops. *Sorry, officer, should've known better, my old man was on the Force.* He smiled in the mirror. *But these kind of people, they're too excitable, know what I mean, they got no control.* He felt the flash flood of rage ballooning out his head. Fucking spik super, filthy bag of scum, he mouthed pleasantly, not wanting to disturb the smile. The smile held, but it took all the pressure his hands could exert, palms cupped over ears, to abort the explosion and compress his skull back to normal size. When the mirror could contain him again, he took out his comb and concentrated on restoring order to his hair.

Even after she had crossed the street and turned her back on it, walking the other way, the tarp stuck in her peripheral vision. A terrible tidiness. Was it true that women didn't jump? It seemed to her she could recall many a back-page headline in modest type: *Woman Jumps* . . . . Perhaps one noted only the falling bodies of one's own sex.

She leaned against the high stone parapet, looking down as from a redoubt on the farthest march of her civilization. The park below, carved into three distinct levels, led by gradual descent, like some hierarchy of hell, to the river. A notable absence of people. The joggers had already come and gone. Only dogs and dog-walkers figured the landscape, and sparsely at this late hour of the morning. No little children at play (she remembered Wendy and Eric, still with the swaybacks and protruding bellies of infancy, rolling over and over down a grassy incline). No lovers on the grass alas (she remembered the pressing presence of Alex's head on her lap, the loverly fingering of his crisp red hair). The mothers were all benched on this upper promenade, distrustful of the weather, or cautious about broken glass, or needing the reassurance of traffic. The lovers sat in parked cars with rolled up windows, a canned sort of privacy, viz. the couple she had just passed: the man behind the wheel explaining, explaining, explaining; the woman beside him a passenger who could neither brake nor steer, staring straight ahead at disaster, tears streaming down her cheeks. A young woman, moist in eye and skin and hair. In time that one too would be transmogrified into an armadillo, adapted to desert, knowing one overriding necessity: conserve all bodily fluids. For a moment she saw herself tapping on the window, calling out cry, cry! like a comedic Jewish mother urging eat, eat! But instead of advice to the lovelorn, "Wendy!" she called out. Having pulled free, the dog seemed headed toward the street with that peculiar sidewinder trot entailed by a dragging leash. In obedience to her command—or more likely such had been his original intent—he stopped at the curb, lifted a leg against a tire, and came sidewinding back. She took a firmer hold on the leather strap, embarrassed to see the driver of the sprayed car still in his seat, combing his hair.

Now why, she would like to ask him, did men always tilt their elbows so awkwardly high when using a comb, giving that simple act as contorted a look as the scribbling of left-handed schoolchildren seated at right-handed desks? And why did they evade frank mirrors, relying instead on mirrors with ulterior motives, like that narrow, ill-positioned one in the car? Or those little swivel sticks left unguarded for a moment on the dentist's tray? Or best of all, no mirror at all, but some chrome embellishment or polished brass fitting or the glass plate of shop windows, the encounter with self maintained as purely adventitious.

She almost laughed aloud—a wifely memory had followed naturally, though it was questionable if as an ex-wife she was entitled to it: Jack playing with a stainless steel knife, lifting mustached upper lip in a snarl, the better to see the reflection of his white teeth. The driver of the car turned his head and caught her smiling, sobered her with his hostile look. His point was taken: no car owner likes dogs to urinate against his tires. She walked resolutely away, asking the city at large what was one supposed to do with males? Not against the tires, the rubber rotted. Not against the trees, the bark suffered. Not against the benches, the sitters objected. Not against those railings, children played there. But unlike bitches, who did their business in a businesslike way, males had to do it *against* something.

Out of winter's habit, she had walked past the steps leading down to the river park, forgetting her promise, but the dog would not have it so. She succumbed to the walleyed look of pleading, the stubborn dragging of the butt. Very well, she impressed on him the mute understanding, they would descend and she would unleash him, once he had done his duty, not before. She stood aside for the file of little hooded figures from St. Andrews, guarded fore and aft by a nun. Donned with those black robes was of course the breastplate of faith, but also a police whistle, she noticed. She watched the orderly descent with a casual pity—poor boys, marched to their games like prisoners lockstepped into an exercise yard for the brief hour required by law. Before descending herself, she checked her coat pocket for the yellow plastic bag with which each day she conscientiously collected the dog's feces. A civic virtue as embarrassing, when viewed by onlookers, as a private vice. Suddenly skeptical of that dragging of the butt—worms again?—she resigned herself to examining the specimen at home.

The double flight of steps offered a descent in opposing directions. She left it up to the dog. He took such an ecstatic plunge to the left that she had to hold on to the rough granite sidewall of the steps, almost hanging him in midair. Her hand remembered the cold graininess of the stone, the broad slope on which the children used to slide, grinding away their hardiest clothes: Wendy in handkerchief-size jumpers, tiny stick legs in wrinkled tights; Eric in macho jeans and Western boots. She had to stop halfway down when the hot flush swept through her like the oceanic aftermath of some volcanic eruption. A fretful "shit!" escaped, a susurrus of despair. And balled in her hand—no handkerchief in the pocket like her mother's, lace-edged, monogrammed, of finest Irish linen—was the plastic bag to hold it all.

The old cunt had smiled at him. He sensed a prearrangement—the curb space provided for his car, the pussy waiting for his cock—not to his liking until he rolled it over, placed himself on top. He set his own conditions: *if* she went below, he would follow. She passed the entrance, ignored the steps. But the dog did not. *If* she took the left flight, he would follow. She descended to the left.

He carefully locked the car and positioned himself against the parapet, from which he could track her progress on the walk below. He threw his head back, shaking the carefully combed hair into free fall, smiling a young man's first-day-of-spring smile, having assumed the missionary position with his own fate. Hand in pocket, he fingered keys, knife, loose change, playing with his godhood, looking down on the dark head now just below him as equally as he eyed the cockroaches that rode his elevator back home. *If* it stops on four (or two or five), he would decide. Those times the elevator shot up express to six, he would get out and let the little bugger live. But when it stopped first on four (or two or five), he brought his foot down hard, effecting the preordained squash.

The flush subsided. Right after her mother's death, she had been equally battered by waves of grief. Shock waves that broke upon her at the most unexpected moments—in the middle of a lecture, at the theater, the supermarket, in Jack's arms—making a shambles of all the little satisfactions of her life. Career, marriage, children—mere flotsam bobbing in a sea of loss. "The shock was the way it happened, one moment she was kissing you good-bye, the next moment she was dead. But you'll get over it," Jack had said hatefully, that bland assurance somehow diminishing her. As if she were dying and he were downplaying the importance of her symptoms. But he was right, she had. Almost had. And so this too—these hot flashes and cold sweats, this maenadic frenzy of the flesh mourning for itself—would in time recede, grow more and more infrequent, less and less intense. Like any love betrayed.

Meanwhile she would have liked a handkerchief, not a plastic bag that left her with a clammy awareness of the scatological content of her days. Half washroom attendant, half sibyl. Start with the children: the daily diapering, the examination of stools for augury. Then came the children's pets. Cat pans to be cleaned, dogs to be walked. Attention must be paid even to mute beasts. Blood in the urine? Worms in the stools? She had thought to be done with looking for signs. But now this latest gift from Wendy, passing through (wearing the jeans now, while Eric sported white lab coats and dangled a stethoscope with an intern's aplomb). Five days at home, just time enough to pick up a stray dog in the park, then on with the knapsack and off again, travel being Wendy's chosen career. Where to? she and Jack had separately asked. Friends in London, they had been told, awaited their daughter eagerly. Friends in Gstadt. Friends in Morocco. She had been struck dumb by the thought of friendship on such a worldwide scale. A conglomerate. An international cartel. I wouldn't buy stock in it, Jack had said.

So here she was, left holding Wendy's dog. Whatever happened to finders, keepers? Sly Wendy, who couldn't settle on a name. To name was to possess. Astute Wendy, who had vigorously rubbed its ears, Jack's hair, her cheek and said good-bye with a gush of generic endearment. Yet she too knew the rules. Wendy's dog it would remain, shortened perforce, for the sake of command, to Wendy herself. Sit, Wendy. Stay, Wendy. The dog obeyed, as the daughter never had, never would. All that was needed was another dog called Eric. Shut up, Eric. A dog would shut up. Not yap long-distance about his concern, with such delicacy of thought as only sons are capable of. "I don't understand this divorce thing, it seems to be an epidemic with women your age." Mad dogs and menopausal women ravaging the countryside. "I wish you would explain what you have in mind." There was never an end to the unreasonable demands of children.

Explain that September. Just two years ago? Yes—she counted now as from a biblical event—Mother died that July. August was laid waste by the legalities of grief, but September came as usual. Suddenly, as usual, all the cars back from the country. The Jews had a better sense of timing—this was when the year began, not during a mid-winter break. Across the street a jam of out-of-staters double-parked for the unpacking of freshmen assigned to Strachey Hall. Girls with jouncing breasts, boys with ungraveled cheeks. How young was young came as a sharper surprise each year. They held their audio equipment in a wide frontal embrace, leaving the nonessentials (clothes, books) to crumpled parents bringing up the rear. So Wendy had lugged her giant stuffed panda every day to nursery school.

"All those TVs and hi-fis. Like looters in a ghetto riot," Jack said, smacking his soft-boiled egg.

She directed him to the implement for precisely cutting off the top. "That will do the job much neater."

"It doesn't call for trepanning. Minor surgery will do."

Explain that morning. Breakfast as usual in the porchlike room, whose casement windows, starting knee-high, let in the full strength of the morning sun. Mother had liked that room. (Mother! The shriek—the rampaging uncomprehending grief—tore through her even now and was gone.) Jack held his cup out, frowning at the news. She had poured his coffee, revising Merrill's lines on middle age: *This is who I am; this is where I live; this is the person I live with; my mother is dead; I will not fall in love again.*

She left the news to Jack, went back to childhood for the true sense of September. The smell of new beginnings. New school tablets with that coarse freckled paper. Pencils sharpened to points so fine they had the rarified air of mandarin uselessness. The pomp and ceremony of new dresses, still stiff with factory sizing. New unscuffed loafers. New books. New resolutions.

An ugly sucking sound, like the fast furious eddy of bathwater down the drain, recalled her to her marriage. Jack, straining his coffee through the bushy overhang of his mustache. At first she had tried just to visualize the upper lip shaven. Had no intention of looking further. But a tight-haunched, tail-twitching compulsion took over, drove her on. She was Fatima, trembling in the knees, fitting the key into the locked door. She was Psyche, holding her breath, lifting the lamp. What face would she see if she unrolled the thin gauze of daily habit and shared property and child-raising cares, the twenty-eight-year limp length of time? A thing of nameless horror? An effulgent god, ravishing in his beauty? Or some Jamesian nightmare—nothing at all?

"What do you think?" Jack had chosen that moment to ask her. "Is it really working?" He was looking doubtfully at the silvery surface of the electric coffee pot, using spread fingers for a comb. Astonishing, she had found it, that Jack, canny as they come, should fall for a TV advertisement. A preparation guaranteed to return grey hair to its former youthful color "so gradually your friends will never know." Dutifully she examined him. There was in fact new color. A faint touch of green, like the iridescent shine on meat going bad.

She knew then that she would leave him. "Yes," she said, feeling pity, wanting to be kind. She had stretched in the sun. Already in her nostrils, the smell of new beginnings.

"I hope you're satisfied," Eric phoned her when Jack remarried.

"Quite," she said.

"Well, it's your own doing," he said. Apparently the distance between them was too great for him to hear her, so yes, she agreed, to keep the call short, she had asked for it. Yes, it was what she had said she wanted. She would have to learn to live alone and like it. Except—

With the discriminating ear of the partially deaf, he heard *except* quite clearly. "Except what?" he demanded.

Except, she was not exactly alone. Wendy had come, Wendy had gone, but she had left behind another damn dog.

Damn dog, indeed. She looked coldly down on the joyous mutt, who had stopped at the bottom of the steps. He sniffed the air, picked up the spoor of freedom, and lifted a galvanic leg against the stone to mark their passing.

From his vantage point he could see all three levels of the park, count the sparse population on the walks, remark the emptiness of benches. Only the playing fields down by the river were peopled. Small boys in red hooded jerseys, white lettering on the back (Saint something—he couldn't make it out) began a soccer game, refereed by a nun. Short shorts and long bare thighs attested an immunity to cold he found as suspect of snobbery as those lettered jerseys, thinking of his Joey still huddling in a ski jacket.

The game was suspect too—all dribbling with the foot and butting with the head. No hands. No crunch of bone on bone. A game for perverts. Aguilar's kid, prancing his fat ass down the dark first-floor hall, kicking a soccer ball. *Pelé, Pelé, Pelé!* Aguilar applauded, slashing out with that spik smile at Edie, who scored by smiling back, then gave it to him in the elevator all the way up. The super's kid in private school, but not Joey, oh no, not Joey. Was he surprised Joey got into trouble? Maybe if she was home all day like Aguilar's fat slob of a wife, stinking up the halls with garlic instead of waiting on tables from 4:00 P.M. to midnight, sprouting varicose veins under fluorescent lights. . . . They rode up in opposite corners, like boxers flexing against the ropes. He eyed her not directly but in the corner mirror fixed at a height to forewarn of muggers in an expectant crouch. He saw the top of her head swollen to ludicrous proportion and the darker ravine of her part. Blonde by nature, she had to be even blonder. That kind of bitch was never satisfied. "*He* don't quit every job he gets, *he*'s got two other buildings he takes care of, works like a dog . . . ."

And filed a complaint with the police, she swore this morning. He should have believed her, if only because of that pursed, mouth-full-of-pins look, as if she were sucking on the satisfaction like a sourball.

What a con job, all that shit about blondes. Without makeup, lashes, brows, her blondeness looked like a congenital disease. She was leaning against the headboard, legs sprawled apart on the unmade bed. Obscene V. But fully dressed in purple slacks and pink nylon turtleneck, under which he could see the spiral construction of her bra, arousing savage thoughts of appearance (real tits) versus reality (half-filled sandbags that swung menacingly over him when she rolled on top, her tit for tat before she allowed him to come at her from behind). Love taps from a weighted cosh.

Aguilar filed a complaint, you betta believe it. He didn't believe it because she was dressed that way, because she was dressed at all. He knew her daytime attire as nightgowns of clammy nylon sheerness, rendered modestly opaque by dirt, trailing a wake of female smells. *Threatened with bodily harm*—she really sucked hard on that official phrase. He would have company if he hung around, she warned; they had promised Aguilar to drop by and have a little talk with him. She was doing the threatening now, he figured shrewdly. She wanted him out. He might not be a big brain, but he knew the answer to that one. Some john was due to walk in through that door the minute he walked out. He could recognize the anticipatory tension of a woman readying herself for intimate inspection. Painting her toes. Cleaning her nails. Sweetening her breath. Leaving the face to last. A shocked look at the clock—did he know the time? Was he trying to get himself fired from yet another job? He grinned. He was not so dumb. He dropped the time bomb then. Already fired, he took pleasure in announcing, as of yesterday. Her compressed lips conveyed an almost alimentary disgust, but no surprise. Then stick around, she challenged him, and explain it to the cops.

He was to explain, how do you like that? he canvassed the dog-walkers, the soccer team, the nun hiking her black skirt up in an athletic crouch. *He,* not that filthy cock-sucker who was supposed to clean the halls. Gripping Joey's shoulders, shaking him like a rat. I'll split your skull in two had been a reasonable response to the lilting Caribbean lament: *I just caught him in the act, pissing on the stairs, this kid of yours, how you expect me to keep the building decent, man, when you tenants act like animals, stinking up the place worse than a zoo?*

His hands tightened on the edge of the parapet as if to vault over, but the white-knuckled tension was retrospective. He was feeling the thin cartilege of an Adam's apple fragile as an eggshell, he was pulling the greasy head back down in the yellow rivulet dripping off the wall: *Smell that, you bastard, that's PR piss. Only PRs and perverts piss in the halls.*

Following down the steps, he was assailed by uriniferous intimations. PRs and perverts. The thought took form but refused to sing.

She followed the upper-level walk, edging away from the stone rampart on her left (rats, not flowers, in the crannied wall). On the street above, she had sensed, but blindly as the dog, some great impending event; here below no one could fail to see the steaming signs of spring—robins and budding shrubs and the marshy look of grass so recently uncrumpled from the weight of snow. Winter, now that it was over, could be graded with a pass. No honors, but it had passed. In committee meetings, in classes, in institutional teas, in departmental dinners. Even private social obligations (that joyless duty-bound word for friends) had been met sufficiently to avoid remark.

To her ever-present craving for solitude, as dissolute and dangerous as an alcoholic's for drink, she had succumbed only for two chartered weeks in December. In mid-flight from Christmas, smiling thank you at the stewardess, she had handled the memory of twenty-eight scraggly pines shared with Jack without a scratch. Never one to cling to faded tinsel glory, no believer in epiphanies, each year she had thrown them out promptly on the first. *Twenty-eight years of marriage, just like that, you throw it out?* Jack's face when she asked for the divorce. Incredulous. Who was the man, of course. No man, she had crowed, as cocky as ever Ulysses.

No man, she had roared, industriously cleaning out the drawers and closets of her life to make room for one. Six months to turn a roar into a whimper. Whimpering still, twenty thousand feet up in the sky: last year, this time, with Alex. Haunted by the Ghost of just one Christmas past, as if the score and more spent with Jack had never been; by the one tree (artificial) that had supplanted a whole forest of green. Last year, this time, Alex. Oh yes! she thanked the stewardess for the tinkling drink. Tinkle, tinkle, mocked the cart, inching its way down the narrow aisle, mimicking Alex's little tree.

Impatient at the unwrapping—so much crushed tissue paper—Alex had taken the package from her, did the job himself. Tinkle, tinkle, went the artifact of crystal, needles of glass.

"The kiddies wouldn't approve, I know, because it's not the real thing, but I wanted to get you something that would last."

Christmas after Christmas seriatim, was the promise of that tinkling. She had twitted him about the sentiment, the better to wallow in it herself.

"But not *kiddies*. Please." She smiled the rebuke but that epithet for undergraduates set her teeth on edge. It was his accommodating way, she sensed, of adding to his years. It served only to remind her how close to kiddiedom he was himself.

She had cut her finger, flicking the needles to set the tree atinkle again. He had drunk her blood.

Still she had survived. Christmas and back. The dregs of winter. Even Jack's call, welcoming her back. He was so pleased the kids had accepted his new wife. *Sonia wants me to tell you what wonderful kids they are. All your doing, she's sure, not mine.* Over the phone she made a polite disclaimer. *They took to Sonia right away, they really like her.* What they really liked (Eric, that is—Wendy didn't count, Wendy liked everyone) was having him off their hands. She stared at the emergency numbers on the wall—fire, police, ambulance, consumer complaints—all posted after Jack had moved out, as if these were the contingencies of life a woman alone need fear. Trying to decipher Wendy's added doodling—the marginal illumination of a medieval text—she heard Jack out. With a plagiarist's low art, he was taking credit for their new lives, applauding his, deploring hers. Had he gone farther afield than his office for her replacement, he might have pulled it off. But she had met his Sonia, knew her well. A mythic concoction, such as resulted from the joining of two separate beasts—blowsy and vulgar from the waist up, elegant and sleek from the waist down. She could see Sonia only in a seated pose, rearranging her legs, making the same play with them that Victorian ladies once had made with hands. Sonia, hysterically afraid of old age at thirty, and now hysterically married, from Jack's account. It tickled her to throw a new slide on the screen:

Sonia as Eric saw her—a practical nurse for a senile, incontinent old man. Eric always looked to the future. But over the phone she was careful not to laugh.

"Hi there. Haven't seen you down here all winter."

She looked up to see dogs first, two Baskerville hounds on ten-foot leashes, pulling in opposite directions, accounting for the man's arm-extended pose of Christ on the way to Calvary. Terrifying beasts, not only leashed but muzzled. She looked at the leather straps and far from being reassured, pictured rending canine teeth and slavering jaws. Then remembered the muzzles were for the dogs' protection, not hers. Poison, their owner had warned her, one dog-lover to another, convinced that the garbage strewn in the park was impregnated with some deadly toxin, a trap deliberately set by some nut who had it in for dogs. She didn't believe it? What about those crazies who put ground glass in candy at Halloween?

"Hello!" she cried with excessive cordiality, atoning for the instinctive urge to turn and run. Here was a practical nurse if ever there was one, this middle-aged son of a man whose name still drew students to the campus although his title had been emeritus for fifteen years, whose presence still lingered in her department, as tantalizing, as malicious as the smile of the Cheshire cat. Better a callous Eric, a careless Wendy than progeny such as this: never married, never even on his own, still at home (his mother had a stronger instinct for self-preservation, absconding many years before). Grown grey in service, as they said of faithful retainers. It occurred to her she had never seen him walking at his own pace. Either he shuffled slowly bearing his father's fragile weight or, as now, plunged forward between two dogs in a drawn-and-quartered gait.

Bravely she stood her ground before the approach of that silly-putty body whose flesh had shape only by virtue of its dress—remove his clothes and it would puddle to the ground. Oh God, she thought, warned by some ambient vision that she was bumping into disaster.

Not liking the look of muzzled dogs, he leaned against a rough-barked tree, hands in the breast-high slits of vinyl jacket, a flying ace waiting to be sent up in the kind of history-dim war movies were made of. The river astounded him. The city of his intimacy was a monoto-

nous landlocked plain. The trees he knew, though nourished with com-
post heaps of garbage, never reached such impressive height. You
ought to bring Joey over some Sunday afternoon, was the advice he
gave himself, then immediately resented, hearing in it the recrimina-
tory echo of Edie's Sunday complaint: *Luke, Luke, that's all I hear, you
spend your day off shooting baskets with that punk friend of yours, but
you ain't got time for your own son.* The echo bounced around inside
his head—*punk friend, punk friend, punk friend*—making his eyes
smart, redden, as if welling with blood.

A clutch at the heart, fingers groping for the pack of cigarettes which
should have been there, confirmed the bitter emptiness of life. The slut,
he thought, but the intonation of the inner voice was flat, uncolored by
emotion, a judge's voice impartially addressing the facts. She had
rifled his pockets, found the pack, tossed it on the bed, and the way she
made a bed, it would still be there under the lumpy cover, shedding its
loose tobacco in the grimy wrinkles of the sheet. Just to follow her to
the bathroom, he had to step over a whole series of stinking panties,
coiled like cow turds on the shag rug. Standing in the doorway, he had
watched her take a final drag, spit her distaste for his brand, flip the
butt into the toilet, then set about the work of making up a face. The
mouth that materialized in the mirror, as lushly poisonous in color as a
tropical growth, answered his suspicious query. Hospital visiting hours
started at eleven, she was off to see Joey. Eyes took shape, drawn in by
crayon. At his mumbled "Oh yeah, I forgot," they rolled upwards.
Speaking eyes that said You hear, God? You hear? as if He were the
tenant on the floor above. He beats up on his own kid, they're taking
X rays right now, and he *forgot.*

Outfoxed again, was the message he decoded in the lashes batted up
and down to test their sticking. Absently, almost gently, he reminded
her that the kid had been peeing in the hall, no kid of his was going to
grow up with a filthy habit like that. The face in the mirror no longer
held him, it was on the drying pantyhose above the shower his attention
was fixed, that limp one-dimensional dark shadow of her crotch. He
drifted off in a cunnilingual fantasy, came to with an image of her head
seized in the V, the ends crossed, pulled tight . . . .

A whistle blew, piercing as a traffic cop's, crying foul. On the field
below, the nun held the ball in the crook of her arm, examining a

muddy knee up for inspection. The kid limped off to sit on a bench and the ball was put back into play. Wandering down the hill, he watched at closer range, revised his estimate of the players' age. Younger than Joey, though equalling him in height. For Joey's sake he felt an accusatory resentment at those aristocratic inches, the cut of their hair, the hardiness of their bare legs, the effluvium of expensiveness that filled their private air even in a public park.

Watching the play, he wondered at kids so young being in a school at all. Some had to give a preliminary skip before achieving a real kick, as if not yet sure which nerve string pulled which leg into the air. And though running hard to meet the ball—he had to laugh out loud—were as apt to duck as to butt hard head against hard ball. The kid on the bench had pulled up his hood, was blubbering over a scratch. Never you mind, Joey, he sent the reassurance winging to his son, who took his punishment like a man, without a sound. You could take on two of them, these little pansies-in-the-making, even with one arm in a cast.

Yet from disdain a certain sympathy sprang for poor buggers attached even on the playing field to a skirt. Manliness was learned from men. The generous impulse which drew him to the bench had a salutory effect, relieving the pressure in his neck, the tightness of his skin. He sat down, for the first time feeling the reality of the sun, seeing clear-eyed that it was spring. Comfortably he put an arm around the huddled red jersey shoulder. "Hey, kid, you gotta learn to take your lumps—"

The sun was blotted out by blackness. He looked up to see under the wimple the clear skin, the clear whites of the eye, the glance cold and blue and sharp as an ice-pick.

"Take your hands off that child. Clear out of here or I will call the police."

Stunned, confused, accepting guilt before he even understood the charge, he moved on automatic pilot, was halfway up the hill before his steps wobbled under the impact of her meaning. He sat down on the nearest bench, scratched where the wristlets of his jacket had ribbed his arm, where the top of socks gripped his calves, where the seam of his crotch threatened suddenly to divide him in half. He heard the whistle again, his whole body reacting with one great swollen itch of shame. He tried the exorcism of obscenity—sucked each other off, they did; got their kicks from a limp-cocked man nailed to a cross—but he could not summon up the necessary faith. The words died in a numb mumble as the red file of sweaty kids headed back to school, bunching together then sliding apart, ordered to keep in line. Black-skirted turn-keys, that's all they were. He turned his head away when he saw their route would take them past his bench, and met the nasty look of the other occupant of the bench. Smash his face in! his pride screamed. His muscles hardened, he felt his body as a great teetering weight ready for lift-off.

"Look at 'em, will you," the old man snarled, rolled newspaper for a pointer. "You'd never guess they're the worst hoodlums in the neigh-borhood. You should see them when they get out of school and them sisters ain't around."

Only a slight lurch betrayed his sudden grounding. A nod of agree-ment, the old fool must have thought, nodding back, spitting his opin-ion on the paved path. "Kids get away with murder nowadays. Look how they coddle them juvenile offenders."

He squeezed out a grunt, thinking of Joey in a hospital bed, for whom he'd done his best. I want the kid should have TV in his room, he had instructed the admitting office. He ought to drop in, make sure he got what he was billed for, but later, when Edie was no longer there. Edie. The name filled his mouth with spittle. At least the kid would have clean sheets for a change. He spat, outdistancing the old man, who gave him a venomous look and snorted that age had nothing to do with it, they ought to be put away for a good long stretch, not let right back out on the street. "The way I look at it, you do a man's job, you get a man's pay."

He tried his voice. "That's a fact." It sounded all right.

A quick glance up the hill showed the two of them with the dogs still yakking away. She looked his way and beneath the impassive skin of his face, the raw red musculature grinned. He had the time, he could wait. He leaned back, spread his legs, opened wide his arms, letting his hands hang limply over the top slat of the bench, and received the sun.

A low growl vibrated in the back of Wendy's throat. "Sorry," she said, pulling her dog out of reach. Wendy was a fighter, she apolo-gized, enjoying a private grin at the sight of his huge beasts straining at the leash, not to attack but to give her little mutt a wider berth.

"Wendy?" With arms all but pulled from the sockets by the two dogs, their master lolled his head to one side. Ah, the crucified has finally expired, she thought. But he was merely examining Wendy's sex. "That name throws me. I keep thinking he's a girl."

"Windy with an i. As in wind. Not fast as, but what he passes." She rather fancied that fake etymology, which spared her any reference to a daughter whose charitable impulses were as fleeting as her visits.

His giggle gave her credit for an off-color joke, which he capped with "They sure do, don't they." Such were the amenities of dog-walkers. Having observed them, she needed only some plausible excuse to hurry on. He was sure to bring the name up. She was cured—tanned and cured—but still she flinched in advance at the sound of Alex's name on those blubbery lips. Our mutual friend, he would say.

"Have you heard from our mutual friend?"

"Alex?" A random guess, a name plucked out of air. No, she had not heard.

"Nor have we." He pouted. Others had. He understood that Alex liked it out there in California. Preferred the warmth and intimacy of a small campus. What a pity his tenure in her department had not come through. "Father still misses him, you know. Our Thursday evenings are not the same. And you—" a mock-accusatory *you* delivered with a knowing thrust—"you have failed us too of late."

So many meetings, so much work—she labored on, piling excuse upon excuse. He understood, he said. She saw the orphan sadness in his eyes and knew he did. For him too Alex had lit up the gloom. "May I come?" Alex had asked, and she had brought him. Her own occasional attendance had been no more than a Confucian observance of respect. Alex had other ends in view. A word from you, sir, in support of my tenure . . . . So kind to the Grand Old Man. And just in case it mattered, almost as kind to the footling son. Who had never mattered. So kind to her too—poor Alex, he had miscalculated there as well. No believer in participatory democracy, in promotion committees, he went right to the top. Chairman of the department, fuck her good. And when the tenure didn't come through—

"Alex—" he began again, but she stopped him with a cry of recognition directed at a bench below. A friend she had arranged to meet—waiting there for her! She must run—regards to his father—so good to see him—good-bye. She took off with a stride of desperate girlish sprightliness, Wendy yapping at her heels, delighted to be on the move again. Behind her was hurled a farewell shout. *Alex!* was all that reached her.

Alex! The name plowed into her, filling her with his presence. Alex with his red beard and wild visionary hair, crackling with energy like a Blake drawing. The hard wiry line of his body. Not to be confused with the hard wiry line of rectitude. *Like they say, you're not getting older, you're just getting better.* She, like Jack, had fallen for a TV commercial. *God, the richness of you.* Gathering in her breasts. *I feel like the king in his counting house.* Chiropractic finger tracing the knobby outline of her spine. *Do you love me?* Parting the sweaty crack. *Do you really love me?* Mapping the inner thigh. *A woman like you?* The finger circling like a hovercraft over her belly, that scarred field of marriage and childbirth, barely brushing the thatch. *God I've been wasting all these years.* Barely brushing, then off again, leaving behind a rictus of agonizing desire. He had wanted to make her grab. And she had grabbed. God, how she had grabbed! The enveloping flush this time came from a door opened on a furnace of shame. To be so used. In company with *that.* That idiot son of greatness, abandoned to his muzzled dogs.

With a tight-voiced "May I?" she inserted herself between the two men on the long bench, looking at neither, her eyes fixed at hand level—a frayed pinstripe sleeve, a black vinyl one. Pinstripe held a newspaper. She inclined her head deferentially, more to the printed word than to the sleeve. A conversational pose, seen from the walk above, allowing her to concentrate on her own hand gripping Wendy's leash. The sallow remnant of winter tan proved her Christmas cure. *I want to die,* had been her hopeless thought as the plane took off from the ice-slicked runway and she held tight to the arms of her seat. But suicide was for the optimistic young. *How well you look,* had been the universal cry when she returned, white middle-aged female fat rendered down to the brown crispness of pork cracklings. But now that the tan was fading, the hand at which she stared looked suddenly withered.

"Damn you, get away," she muttered to the dog, who had laid his head athwart her knees, the better to beseech her for more running, less sitting. A glance up the hill showed her it would be impolitic to move as yet. There he still was, at the base of the stone steps, a ludicrous Laocoon entangled with the long leather leashes. His dogs were refusing to mount. "Go play by yourself," she commanded, and unsnapped Wendy.

"Better watch it, the cops are out in full force today." It was pinstripe speaking. "I seen them give two tickets already for dogs off the leash. That's what I call cracking down on crime." The man exuded bitterness like a body odor. She moved slightly away, encroaching on the space of the other man, asked his pardon. "All the rapes, murders, muggings up there on the street, and they're down here cleaning up the park. You know why, don't you?"

She kept her eye on the exit above. Slowly the dogs were being hauled up. Responding to the pinstripe sleeve, she ventured the guess that there had been complaints.

Complaints? The word was hurled back to her, a hard smash of scorn returning her weak serve. "My place was broken into twice, just this last month. You think I didn't complain? You think they gave a shit— excuse me, lady, but that's not the way it works. Now if you live in one of them buildings up there on the Drive, and you step in it—that's a different story. Then they listen to you, you complain."

Man and hounds had disappeared, unchaining her from this ticklish perch. She looked about for Wendy, caught sight of him behind a distant row of bushes. That unmistakable hunched posture called her to her duty. "Excuse me," she said gladly. Even the collection of stools was less distasteful than such conversation as this man afforded.

A little loose—worms? she questioned again—but still collectible with a practiced swipe. Thank heavens for small favors, as her mother used to say. What if Wendy had brought home a Great Dane? Shuddering at the thought, she looked almost fondly at the mutt, threw him a stick. He chased it, brought it halfway back, then reverted to puppyhood, crouching, stick in mouth, semaphoring with his tail a juvenile challenge: catch me if you can. "Oh, I will," she threatened with a semblance of gaity. She chased him through the bushes, past the empty tennis courts, into the memorial grove of trees planted at the end of World War I, crying "I'll catch you, oh yes, I'll catch you," her laugh rattling around in the emptiness at her core.

"Betcha she's one of *them*," the old man sneered with a jerk of the head toward the red brick and creamy stone that rimmed the park.

"Yeah," he said, getting up with the same dulled resentful grunt he gave Edie when she kicked him out of bed for another day of work. "Sure," he said to the dribble from the old fool's mouth which he no longer heard. He walked away, his legs heavy, his body gravid with some weighty impulse. Heft without purpose. He leaned against a tree, watching the show put on by the woman with the dog, his hand in pocket aimlessly tearing cardboard into shreds. Fingers stopped their play. Ticket stubs to the crucial play-off game. Scalper's prices, he had paid. *This is on me*—his very words. But after the game, at the bar, it was Luke's, "Hey, man, put that away," the grip on his wrist forcing his wallet back. They talked, stroking their steins. Above their heads, the flicker of blurred images on the tilted TV. Like a closed-circuit security system, Luke had cracked, making him laugh. Everything Luke said made him laugh. He caught sight of his laugh in the bar mirror, imprisoned behind the whiskey bottles, and for a moment could lay no claim to it. A moment of panic. Evicted from his own face. Then Luke told a joke about the Polish pope and his body unclenched, like a fist uncurling.

"Where you been? You know the time?" Edie screeched when he rolled in, feeling no pain.

"Where've I been? I ate out, that's all. Boiled tits and fried pussy. Home cooking like I don't get at home," he jeered.

"Where you been?" they asked the minute he walked in. "Get your ass right upstairs—they been asking for you." Fifteen minutes late to work, they call him on the carpet. So he thought. He had looked around for Luke to nudge, to slap, to touch a friend like a hunchback's hump for luck, to say as an excuse, "Some game last night, man oh man." No Luke. One beer too many. Sleeping it off. So he thought.

Memory was an agonizing cramp, shutting off the flow of blood, shooting needles in his chest. He stood. They sat. Papers passed between them. They spoke only to each other.

"Just petty pilfering, Corelli says."

"Corelli's sure of that?"

"Yeah, a loner. No connection with them three big-time operators. Too dumb to even know what was going on. It's there on page three."

Pages turned. "He brags about that little Sony he took home—" a short bark of laughter, the punctuation of contempt—"and right under his nose they were stealing wholesale, robbing us blind."

"Under our nose too, Jesus Christ." The cigar bobbed up and down between clamped jaws. "Okay, I agree with Corelli. A waste of time. We hooked the big fish, that's what counts. We'll throw the little one back in."

They didn't let him say a word. He was fired, out the door, still trying to fit in a hey, hey, what's going on. Too dumb to know. Back in the stockroom he announced that he had quit, he had had it up to here. Clearing out his locker, he still had to ask himself which one was the company plant, that fink Corelli. The answer came with the slamming of the metal door. Up and down the empty corridor he heard the reverberating twang: *punk friend, punk friend, punk friend.*

The moist earth sucked in his feet, let go with a plop like the parting of blubbery lips. The dog barked hysterically. The woman caught him, took away his stick, shrieked with laughter.

She raised her arm to throw the stick—"just once more," she told the dog—and brushed against the low branch of a tree. On the back of her hand, the sticky imprint of its pubescence. She looked out on the hazy shimmer of the river. The whole world ached with spring, a tender ache, like a young girl's breasts. *Mother!* The memory broke from her like a cry. Hand in hand, they had stood together on this very spot. The shade was July-thick then, the leaves their ultimate green. She smiled, remembering how her mother honored all occasions by her dress, a woman who would abandon last decorum. That day she had donned her "walking shoes"—summer-white, heels a good three inches high, turning the ankle perilously on uneven ground, but with a fringed flap (vestigial reminder of Indians padding through the forest in deerskin moccasins?) that to her mother signified comfort. "Such nice trees," her mother said, a mere politeness, addressed more to them than to her. Even communing with nature, her mother had only small talk. So she had thought. But then she saw her mother's eyes. They were filled with tears. Like the feigning lady of Bazille, she had suddenly thought, struggling to find words for her new fondness, borrowing Wilbur's instead: *And when with social smile and formal dress, She teaches leaves to curtsy and quadrille, I think there are most tigers in the wood.*

How dear a habit now, this grief. She did not want to lose it, the one remaining tie that held her mother to this earth, that remembered her to these trees. She closed her eyes, the better to hold on. A mother dying in her daughter's arms—now there's a decorous death. But beneath her lids, even her mother mocked her, dying for her benefit all over again, down to the final moment of convulsive vomiting, the explosive emptying of bowels, as if death required a complete evacuation before it took over. One kneels before a dying parent, one expects a blessing. She let go and opened her eyes and hurled the stick not in a playful arc but on a straight vicious path of flight, aimed at all love, all grief.

"That's it," she said with finality, watching the last antic chase. She opened her mouth to call, had time to feel only the faintest skin-prick of forewarning before she was seized from behind. An arm pressed like a crowbar against her windpipe. A front melded itself to her back, interlocking them like jigsaw pieces. She bit into the bunched fabric of a sleeve, her teeth slid off cold slick vinyl. All her blood seemed awash in her ears, yet she heard the delicate click before the pressure of the arm gave way to the tickle of steel.

Even before the tumescence he felt the pain, the knife stabs in the groin. It was from the pain he sought relief, intent on tearing, scraping, ramming, battering, gouging. It was an annihilation he craved, the final explosion of mushroom tip into mushroom cloud.

More incredible than the knife at her throat was the tearing pull on her slacks, the soft crooning obscenities tongued in her ear. A hoot of hysteria pushed against the cold constriction of her throat: I'm through with that, I said that's all, didn't you hear? A dog barked furiously. The universe contracted, expanded, contracted, expanded, even as the dog's barking seemed close, seemed far, approached, receded. He lunged sideways. She felt rather than saw the underbelly kick, heard the shrill yapping tail into the distance. A dog who fights only his own kind, she cursed bitterly. But still a distraction, pulling the knife off line, loosening the wrestler's lock. She twisted half-free.

Okay, he mocked the ogling eyes, you asked for it.

Wendy! she screamed—as once she had screamed for a little girl lost in the park—and saw for the first time the man's face, all the more terrifying for its familiarity. She thought: I know you. She began to pass her whole life in review, seeking to recover his name. And all the while she flailed at the face with the only object she had in hand— Wendy's bag. Its limpness confirmed her sense of nightmarish impotence.

He did not bother to turn his head aside, contemptuous of such an ineffectual plastic slap. The smell struck him just before the seam split. In his eyes, up his nostrils, lumping on his tongue. They were both covered with it, he trying to hawk it up out of his throat, she shuddering with disgust at her hands, when the police arrived, looking for the owner of a dog off its leash fouling the footpaths of the park.

Depression Glass

It was green. It was pink. Or left untinted in the hope of mimicking by machine the elegance of hand-cut crystal. Designs as lushly convoluted as the private parts of certain flowers. Cereal bowls with Shirley Temple surfacing like a drowned moppet as one lapped up the last sweet dregs of milk. Free with box coupons or Friday night at the movies. Today's collectible. Not my cup of tea but a friend of mine is crazy for it, which is why I came back from the flea market with a pink sugar bowl and creamer.

I should have known better than to show them to my father. Woolworth's used to sell that stuff, he sneered; for two ninety-eight you could get a service for twelve. In fact, he had given his mother a set like that—a birthday present—when he was just a kid. Eighty-eight dishes and three big bowls, he said with a shift of discomfort. I was reminded that he was having some kind of prostate trouble.

Now that age is nibbling at his edges, I am trying to be kinder. Three whole dollars, I clucked to show I was suitably impressed. That must have been a fortune to a small boy in the Depression. Oh yes, the Depression, he said. The thought of hard times unmistakably cheered him. For kids, he said, it wasn't so bad; he wouldn't want to be a kid today. Of course, for grown-ups it was different.

In those days, my father said, we were as two nations, between whom there was no intercourse and no sympathy, who were as ignorant of each other's habits, thoughts, and feelings as if we were dwellers in different zones, or inhabitants of different planets, who were formed by a different breeding, were fed by a different food, were ordered by different manners, and were not governed by the same laws. That's merely the gist of what he said, of course, although unlike Disraeli he was distinguishing between the generations, not the rich and poor. Nor was there a cutting edge to his voice, but a softer burr, the throatiness that nostalgia lends when the story is of empire at its crest, or childhood happy, long ago. I've heard it all before.

In those days, my father really said, kids had nothing to do with grown-ups. Except to come home to supper. And do what they were told. And show respect. Not that there was much a boy could do, with grown men begging for any kind of job. Maybe a little yard work, nothing *in*doors, you understand, that was for girls. (He spoke of his sister—sometimes with pity, sometimes with contempt—as of a captured member of the tribe.) And not much of that, he said with a grin that harked back fifty years. Boys knew better than to hang around the house.

As soon as school was out—all day long in summer—he was a member of a pack, playing games on railroad tracks, foraging in woods like feral beasts reverting to their natural habitat. In towns that size, my father said, streets and sidewalks came to an abrupt stop, as if the money had suddenly given out, and beyond were always woods.

Even when trapped indoors by weather or the night, children kept themselves apart, migrating to back porch, attic, or cellar, anywhere no grown-ups were. So far he could recollect, they shared the same room only for meals or listening to the radio—those comedy hours—or when company came and progeny were displayed along with the few pieces of good china. Even then, after their growth was measured, their learning tested, they were released like cattle from a barn. Go out and play, they would be told. And—too late—don't slam the door.

Oh yes, I had heard all that before. So have my kids. They hate it when they have to visit him every other August. Go out and play, he demands. Play *what*, they ask. His idea of entertainment, they report, is to watch the Perseids (shooting stars, he calls them, which they find quaint). He doesn't realize that standing knee-high in wet grass, being eaten up alive, can't compete with sky shows at the planetarium. When his turn comes to visit us, they are relieved.

As much for them as for me, I felt a certain resistance should be offered to that idyllic portrait of his youth. Where were the breadlines,

I asked, the apple-sellers, the bonus marchers, the shantyvilles, the Appalachian squalor spreading over an entire land like the fine grey ash of a volcanic eruption? Was the Great Depression then but another fable, a Hollywood invention, just a showcase for William Powell's charm in *My Man Godfrey,* a movie which my kids adore?

Hard times for grown-ups, my father blithely agreed. That same year, when he was eight, he won a prize in Sunday School. A book with pictures, Bible stories told for children. One picture he remembered yet: Adam leaving the Garden of Eden. It had the charm of the familiar, he knew all about evictions. In those days, it was not uncommon to find the sidewalk littered with the insides of a house ripped out like guts from a plucked chicken—the bailiffs tossed things out any old way. His mother would drag him to the other side of the street, turning her head, nostrils pinched as if the smell was bad, her grip a painful squeeze, just as she had when they once passed a young man exposing himself. My father chuckled. Nonpayment of rent, he confessed, still seemed to him obscene.

Adam hadn't paid his rent, was how he read that picture. And the bailiff was the angel, a powerful henchman with muscular wings, arms folded across a hairless muscular chest. A regular Mr. Clean. As for Adam, my father said, he was getting his just desserts, you could tell by the defeated shoulders and humbled head. Adam after the Fall, that was the title under the picture. And Adam after the Fall, that was how he saw his father. Laid off again, he would nudge his sister, watching the poor guy come up the steps, before the door was even opened. My father, who has worked for the same company for forty years, said "poor guy" with the same mix of contempt and pity I had thought he reserved for girls.

Adam after the Fall. But in that picture, where was Eve? I assumed that, as efficient cause, she shared his shame.

Mother? My father laughed. His laugh shows the too-even bite of false teeth. He was in his thirties when he lost his own, but the union pays for his new sets and every other year he trades them in the way people used to trade in cars. Somehow, he said, he never saw his mother as Eve. More like the bailiff-angel. Both, he suspected, knew only one refrain: You've only yourself to blame. God knows, he and

his sister—your Aunt Helen, he usually adds, forever introducing her—
were so advised on enough occasions.

So when his father came home, the hour too early, he and his sister
knew what was coming. Laid off again. And only himself to blame.
(My father was in high spirits—he laughed again.) When his mother
finally died, there were the two stones, side by side: his father's already
weathered smooth, his mother's granite raw and grainy. He had suggested to his sister that one should read Laid Off Again, and the other,
You've Only Yourself to Blame. But his sister—your Aunt Helen, he
reminded me—never had a sense of humor.

Like his sister—my Aunt Helen—I reproved him. No use pretending
he hadn't loved his mother when he had spent all that money—a child's
fortune it must have been—for her birthday present. But my father
never speaks of love. When he leaves he will turn at the door and say,
take that! in the gruff tone of a man delivering a friendly blow to the
solar plexis. And I will take it, the wad of green bills crumpled like
Kleenex that he stuffs into my hand. I no longer need it, but I take it—
what else has he to give?

My father changed the subject, and for the first time asked about the
dog. As if he had just missed him. I told him the dog had reached an
incontinent old age, had to be put away. That he should look so stricken
came as a surprise. So far as I could tell, he had been no more recep-
tive to canine demonstrations of affection than to my own. All the
interest he had shown was in the cost of upkeep, how long a bag of dog
chow lasted, what was the weekly total for the supplement of raw meat.
True, he assumed the role of dog-walker on his brief visits, but it was
the role he found attractive, not the dog. So I had always thought.
There are certain people who are gentry in my father's eyes (although
of course he does not use that word) and they always own a dog.

He had owned a dog once, he told me then in a lachrymose way I
found distasteful. I used the pretext of too much sun to move my chair
away. I have my memories too—like the time we went into the visitors'
room so that he could smoke, and the nurse came in and called his
name. He knew as well as I that mother had just died. But did he cry?
True to his creed—waste not, want not—he pinched out the cigarette he
had just lit, put it back in the pack, stowed the pack in his breast pocket

before he even made a move to rise. And then he wished the woman in the neighboring chair the best of luck. Besides, he lied. It was not owning a dog to bring home a stray and have to get rid of it the very same day.

I had heard that story, I said. The impatience was to let him know I had no wish to hear it again. His mother had had a fit, so the story went. Her face had grown so puffy and so red, so engorged with rage, it had scared him out of a full year's growth. (My father had several such expressions to account for his lack of height, for all his sons being taller by a head.) Don't you ever bring me another mouth to feed, she had screamed. A pity, he would then complain, he had to marry a woman—your mother, I half-expected him to add—whose face turned just as red and puffy when he brought home a dog for his own kids, so of course it couldn't stay. An allergy, the doctor said, but he used to tell me confidentially it was all in her mind.

I had heard all his stories. Too many times. Stories not so much of want and deprivation as of the spartan virtues that flourished in such harsh soil. We knew them well—we his children with our vast estate of toys. He was a generous parent, but all his gifts came wrapped in homilies. In his day, he would say, kids had a self-sufficiency in play. Take two wooden clothespins and a rubber band, you had a gun. With an old inner tube, what couldn't you do. In those days you went *outside* to play. In those days, we gathered, games were neolithic, requiring only sticks and stones.

To my relief, before he started in again, my friend arrived. She had come around to the patio in back where we were sunning to complain that no one had heard the doorbell ring. Barely ten minutes had elapsed since I telephoned, catching her in the pool. I should have known that, hearing the words "Depression glass," she would come just as she was, dripping chlorinated water on the white seat of her Porsche. Such is the collector's ardor. In his sling seat, my father was at eye-level with her navel. He is not at his best with young women in bikinis. My father, I said, pretending to forget they had met the night before. That brought him to his feet. My friend would have settled down for a polite chat, but I hustled her inside before he turned jovial and started telling jokes. He has two kinds of jokes, what he calls his club-car and his parlor jokes. And in the presence of a lady so undressed (we are all ladies, even whores are ladies of the night), I knew which he would choose to tell.

Now that they were gone, he could feel his crotch. The sun felt fine. It seeped in through closed lids, like blood dissolving in a bath. Hot pink. The pink of that glass was different—cool, medicinal. It made him think of the large jars of colored water in Solomon's drugstore window.

There was the pink, there was the green—hard to choose. And colors had a code he wasn't sure he understood. Purple was for old ladies—or was it kings? Red was loud, his mother said. You had to be careful, certain colors had a bad name. Yellow coward. And green—look at him, he's green with envy just because his baby sister got a toy. That's a lie, he said, he didn't give a shoot for ten-cent toys. His mother slapped him in the face to teach him grown-ups didn't lie. But he was eight years old, he had a buttoned fly, from then on when he got a present it was clothes. Helen, nothing but a baby, got a celluloid doll with arms connected by rubber bands strung through shoulder holes. He showed her how you could swing them all the way around like the propeller on a plane. The rubber broke, Helen cried, his mother swatted him again.

That summer even Helen had to go without. Ten cents was trolley fare to the hospital and back. Kids were not allowed, his mother had to go alone. You take care of baby sister now. But no kid with a buttoned fly could afford to play with girls. Ditching Helen became the game. He pounded down a stretch of tarry pavement melting in the heat until the road turned suddenly into dirt. *There* was a feeling to remember— dirt so thick and silky, the finest silt between his toes, an unguent to bare feet. Then off across rougher ground, abandoned fields—the soil as rusty as the sagging barbed-wire fences—to join the others at the sawmill. It had closed down but had left behind a sawdust mountain great to climb.

His dad was working now, Whitey Medford bragged. My dad is dying, he had bragged.

What's a carbuncle, he had to ask his mother. It sounded black as coal, hard and shiny as a diamond, maybe something else to brag about. But it was nothing but a boil. Everyone had boils. He woke up one night and caught his mother out on the porch, all by herself, having a quiet conversation. Dear God, she was saying, dear God. He was surprised they were on speaking terms. Where is God, he had asked her when he was very little, hearing on the radio he must find the Lord. She was hanging up the wash, clothespins in her mouth. Annoyed, that was her look. As if the question wasn't worth the bother of taking clothespins out. How should *I* know, she had snapped, ask your father. For the answer to foolish questions, she always sent him to his father.

A miracle, the doctors called it. They had to make do with miracles then. His father was home again, skin baggy as a hand-me-down. Things will get better now, his mother said. But first his father had to get his strength back. It seemed to him that summer he was always running to the drugstore for another bottle of the tonic that would give his father back his strength.

The important thing is we're all together, his mother said. She wasn't herself that summer, he never once heard her say who was to blame. Where they got the money for all that tonic, he'd never know. Food got a little low but one thing he was sure of, they were never on relief. Those days people had their pride. And knew enough to put away a little for a rainy day. Of course when his mother sighed and guessed she'd have to dig into the bank, she didn't mean a real bank—the kind that failed. She meant the double-knotted handkerchief pinned to her brassiere. Shifting from foot to foot, anxious to get the errand over with, he would watch her fingers fumble with the clasp and see revealed the white swatch of sturdy cotton that bound her breasts. Not like the see-through things they wear today. More like a surgical truss.

That young woman who collected glass, he could see the nipples sticking out.

What was taking them so long? A nice talk with his daughter, and *she* had to come along. And tomorrow he'd be gone. His children never listened when they were growing up. Those days, he'd begin—and immediately they would look ashamed, embarrassed. He could understand if he beat on them with hard-luck stories. There were some guys at work: *What you beefing about, you kids think you got it tough, let me tell you, sonny, what tough is really like.* They never heard that from him. Tough was now, not then.

Why didn't you tell her how you got the money for the glass?

He stirred in his chair, eased his crotch, decided to ignore that carping voice. After all, he didn't steal it, it wasn't a crime, for God's sake he was only eight years old. Some other time he'd tell her, make it a funny story. It *was* a funny story. Eighty-eight dishes, his father said. His mother added, And three large bowls. How they laughed.

That was the point. Hard times or not, people knew how to enjoy themselves. Especially kids. Especially in summer. To walk into the house was like entering a cave, the shades drawn, so dark you had to stand still until you could see again, so quiet you could believe it uninhabited. No loud rows like what went on next door, the neighbors yelling at their grown-up son for just lying around the house, no longer even looking for a job. We come of better stock, his mother said, lowering her voice. That was another reason to stay outdoors, you could make noise. The only rule: you come back when it gets dark.

Dark was when they turned the street lights on, and come summer that could be as late as nine o'clock. Even then he and Helen hung out on the porch, no school tomorrow, counting shooting stars with their father in his flannel bathrobe, its matted nap worn down like the back hair on the elbow of that old dog. Poor old dog. It was August, the right month for shooting stars, and you would think, from the way his father acted, it was an entertainment arranged by him especially for his two kids. Better than a picture show, his father said, though at the time he and Helen would have rather seen Tom Mix. Whenever his father thought they were losing interest, he would promise that one of these days one of those things would hit the earth.

They are sitting that way on the steps of the porch, Helen sound asleep in Father's lap. There are just the two of them now—he and Father—looking up at the sky. He finds it a little scary, the sky so black, so many stars.

Makes you feel little, Father says with respect. But that's why he finds it scary, he's too little as it is.

Did you know—out of the blue, Father asks—your mother's birthday is next Tuesday? Forty years old. What'll we give her for a birthday present?

I don't know, is all he can think of. Only kids have birthdays, he has always thought. And what kind of presents are there but toys, which by the time you are eight you're too old for.

The screen door creaks. They know she is there behind them.

There goes one, Mary, make a wish, maybe it'll come true, Father says. He is joking.

A trip to the moon, Mother wishes.

There's another, Father says. Wish again, a real one.

A trip to Chicago, to see the World's Fair.

That's a good one, Father says, I'd like to see that myself.

I know what you'd like to see, Mother says, that fool woman, naked as a jaybird, swishing her fans.

His father never did get to see Sally Rand. Nor his mother a trip to the moon. Pressed glass, that's what she got, service for twelve. The things you remember. The lady at Woolworth's behind the counter, paying him no mind. He had to pull the purse out and show her he had money.

Pink or green, which had he chosen? The things you forget. A present for his mother, he couldn't help bragging, and before he knew it, he was rooting in a pastureland of hips, blinking in a mist of flowered voile. She had come around the counter to give him a hug. You could trace the corset's skeleton through those summer dresses, sheer as curtain stuff, even through the starchy whiteness of the slip. An anatomical marvel, second only to the fingerbones of a bat.

Pink or green, whichever, the purchase of that gift left him with an empty purse but free, he hoped, of guilt. In those days, you knew right from wrong. Take his own daughter, age fourteen, in tight blue jeans and tighter shoes with four-inch heels on which she pranced, one-toed and hard-hoofed and as oddly gaited as a Tennessee walking horse. Shoplifting was just a lark. They all did it, was her excuse. They all had money, but that was a bore. A thrill they wanted, a thrill they got— the police saw to that—but they would never know a thrill like the thrill of picking up that purse. He could feel it even now in his hand—the worn cracked leather, the burr of corrosion on the metal clasp—as if it were imprinted in the whorls of his fingertips.

It was the kind of purse ladies used for change, and its limpness was kind of sad. He opened it and grew bug-eyed when it saw what it contained. He had found pennies before, a nickel now and then. Once he had fished up a quarter through the street grating. For that you used chewing gum on the end of a stick—a kind of early toolmaking like those chimps they showed on TV. But this was paper money, real dollar bills, rolled up as tightly as the cigs J. J. made on his father's home machine.

He didn't steal it—he would make that clear—it was just found. He always checked the pay phone at the drugstore while Mr. Solomon made up his father's tonic. Nothing in the coin return, as usual, but on a little shelf, the purse.

All the way home he ran, arguing in advance against what he knew his mother would say. He'd have to give it back, she would say. Who would say that today? But with no name inside, they'd *have* to keep it. *She* would keep it, it dawned on him just as he reached the house. A fortune in his pocket and all it would come to was a sack of groceries or the light bill paid and if he got a present, it would be a pair of shoes.

Here's the tonic, was all he said. His hand in his pocket squeezed the purse as if to keep it quiet. She looked at him as if she knew. You're a good boy, she said, but there was no need to run so hard. From the way she kept looking, he knew she knew. Take you hand out of your pocket, she said. If he had been a thief, he couldn't have felt worse. I forgot, he said, that old weak excuse. She looked disgusted. It was like a night-mare, his fist stayed clenched, his hand was stuck. He didn't under-stand why she turned so red, as if the shame was hers, until she issued that command. Stop playing with yourself, she said, and quickly left the room.

Greed, that was his crime. All mine, all mine. What came over him, he'd never know. We must all hang together or we'll hang separately, his mother said every other day or so. He was in high school before he learned it was the Continental Congress Franklin was addressing, not the members of his family. Six dollar bills—no share and share alike, all his—counted in his private quarters underneath the house, a crawl space walled in by a wooden lattice that threw a crisscross pattern of light and shade. It was the one place Helen never followed. Ugh, she shuddered, all those bugs.

What he had there was an orgy—no other way to describe it. A dozen five-cent candy bars—a dozen, count 'em! Which he did, over and over, until the chocolate melted in the wrappers, and he had to lick it

off. Not to mention all those toys he wished he'd had before he got too
old. Like the early Christians in the catacombs, he performed his wor-
ship underground. That was more what it was like than play—the toys
spread out before him like on an altar. A cap pistol with enough pink
rolls of caps to outlast any war. A Junior Carpenter set of tools—
hammer and saw and screwdriver and pliers, too small to be of any
use, each fitted into its own slot in the cardboard backing. It wasn't the
tools so much he liked as the idea of a set. Kids like sets. The Lincoln
Logs in a box shaped like the cabin he was supposed to build, to open
which you took off the roof. But the pistol could not be fired, they
would hear it in the house. And what could he find, in that cramped
space, to hammer and saw? As for cabin-building, the light was so poor
he could hardly make out the notches on the logs to fit them together.
Mostly he sat there, hearing overhead his mother's sharp heels, his
father's slippered shuffle, his sister always on the run, trying to guess
what they were doing as they moved about, or what they were saying as
their voices faded, grew stronger, faded, like bad tuning on the radio.
Even now, basking in the sun, the smell that flared his nostrils was that
of underground, a dark dry excavation of some ancient civilization.
Perhaps the house was still standing, the toys still there, miraculously
preserved in the lava flow of time.

Money was real money then. With all that spending, the purse not
empty yet. It had grown fatter, in fact, like a trick played by an evil
sorcerer, since what remained was all in change, weighing him down.
The night they watched the shooting stars, a great light descended. His
stomach ached, he wanted to be good. Those days, everyone (with the
possible exception of his mother) still had their faith. They believed in
God and that crime didn't pay. Crime didn't pay, he could vouch for
that. With the money he had left, he resolved to buy a birthday present
for his mother. Just the resolve made him feel clean inside. He could
hardly wait until he died, knowing Jesus would pat his head and say
"good boy" the way you praised a dog.

All those dishes. Sheer number must have been the reason for his
choice. Whatever it is, kids like a lot. He had to borrow J. J.'s toy
wagon to carry them home. It was a miracle he could stash them under
the house with no one seeing, not even snoopy Helen. Waiting for
Tuesday was the hardest part. Whenever he could, he would crawl

below and admire the fancy wrapping. Usually they charged for that, the lady behind the counter said, but for a boy who loved his mother so, she did it all for nothing.

Tuesday morning. He ran out of the house still in his underwear. Through the screen door, his mother screamed for him to get right back inside. But when she saw what he was lugging up the steps, she stopped screaming. She didn't get her breath back until the pile of dishes on the table began to grow. Where did he get the money, she wanted to know. He was ready for that—oh he was cunning. Cutting grass, he said, all summer long he had been saving up. In case she asked how come she never saw him pushing anybody's mower, he had that answer ready too. He had to go to the other side of town, he planned to say, where there were front yards so big you couldn't see the houses from the road. J. J. had told him that, bragging how much he made, bragging he was taller. They wouldn't hire a shrimp like him, he was told when he asked to come along.

But his mother had no more questions. Instead she cried. Not noisily—we come of better stock, she may have meant to show—without a sound. Like in those moving pictures before the talkies came. Helen reached up to the table, dropped a plate. The shattering glass brought his father to his feet, his bathrobe clutched, a boxer heading for the ring. Helen whined she couldn't help it, it just slipped out of her hands—the way she always put it, every object acted on its own. No one paid her any mind. Could someone tell him, his father shouted—shh! his mother tugged at the robe—could someone tell him, his father asked more quietly but rolling his eyes about, asking now the sink, now the icebox, now the linoleum, now the oilcloth on the table—could someone please tell him what they were supposed to do with eighty-eight dishes and three big bowls? Shh! his mother said again and his father shut up. It was clear they had never seen so many dishes in their life. His mother kissed him, smoothed his hair back from his forehead with her palm, the way she used to before Helen came along. He squirmed away, he was too old for that. If she was so pleased, why was she crying. Her tears, she said, were tears of happiness. He wondered how you could tell.

That night he broke out in a rash, which he figured was the measles. Measles were going around just then, something was always going around, as he remembered. As it turned out, he never caught the measles—it was whooping cough that almost did him in—so it was probably all that candy. The first and only time he broke out from eating candy. If that didn't prove it was all in the mind, he didn't know what did.

He must have been in a pretty bad state to get out of bed and go looking for his mother, feeling as he did that rooms slept like animals, with a furry breathing life of their own. He started for the other bedroom, but then he saw the light under the kitchen door. He knew those voices. Mother's voice. Father's voice. Familiar voices, but they did not sound the same. They were the voices parents had when their children were asleep in bed.

What could he have been thinking of, to feel a shiver of pure dread? Something to do with fairy tales, was his guess. The best kind of children's books, he argued to this day, but it was true they didn't help you brave the dark. From what he remembered, the strange things that happened all happened in the middle of the night—frogs into princes, princes into frogs, that kind of stuff.

He might not know what lay behind that swinging door, man or beast, but he knew just how far he could push it before the hinges squeaked. Through the crack he could see his mother and his father at the kitchen table. In their usual forms, that was a relief. They were positioned as opponents and in his father's hand the deck of cards was being shuffled with such a flourish, it could only mean a magic trick was about to be performed. Then came the incantation. Eighty-eight dishes and three big bowls, his father chanted—an abracadabra that transformed them in a trice (that was the unit of time all fairy tales employed.) It was a seizure, a fit—that crazy laughter that kept them jerking helplessly about. The kind of fit from which, according to the Brothers Grimm, they would be released only when a fiddle stopped playing or some magic word was pronounced.

Dishes, dishes everywhere, his father chanted. And not a drop to eat, his mother cried, keeping the same beat. Not the right spell for they only laughed the harder. His father, roaring, teetered back on the hind legs of his chair, and his mother shrieked, holding her hand to her chest, the fingers splayed as if, like the frog-prince's servant, she wore three bands of iron around her heart which were about to snap apart.

The things you remember. He went back to bed, unheard, unseen, and by morning, the rash was gone. But not the knowledge that he had looked at them without their knowing. It stuck in his mind. Primal trauma. What they were talking about the night before, those neighbors of his daughter, who thought he didn't know what it meant so they explained. One thing hadn't changed, they still fell back on sex to liven up a party. He had been reminded of a joke—two niggers was the way he heard it, he made it hillbillies so as not to offend—but his daughter shut him up. Be as dirty as you like, it seemed, just don't be funny. He knew now what he should have said. That's no trauma, he should have said. When you wake up in the middle of the night and catch them laughing, that's trauma, he should have said.

It took forever to get rid of my friend. She was excessively grateful for the cream-and-sugar set, but could not resist telling me what I should know before I bought anything like that again. American Sweetheart was the pattern, very rare in red, not worth much in pink, and she was dying for a cold drink. I finally had to mention it was getting late, my kids were waiting to be picked up from their tennis lesson. She just loved my father, she said on leaving (she might have still been talking of Depression glass). Such a funny man. So in spite of my best efforts the night before, he had gotten off a joke or two. The life of the party.

Another sign my father is getting old—left alone, he catnaps. Just like the dog. When my mother died, I hated him, wished it were he instead. Like all those foolish wishes in a fairy tale, it's coming true and I must waste another wishing it away. Not to awaken him, I moved off the flagstone and walked on the grass. But he was not asleep. Did my friend like the glass, he asked without opening his eyes. She was ecstatic, I reported. I would have him know those artifacts of the Depression were as seriously collected as high art.

We sat there a moment in comfortable silence, enjoying the coolness of the house's growing shadow. In those days, he said—as if there had been no interruption, no visitor, I had never left his side—people had so little but they were happy. A surprising statement from a man like him. Ask me to describe my father in one word and I would say, bitter.

Local Habitations

In the first flush of consciousness, while the mind took inventory, defined extremities, reset limits learned in infancy, she was aware of something missing. What that could be was hardly worrisome, warranting no strain to recall, merely an idle stretching of the mind, a cerebral yawn. A matter of small wonderment, soon forgot.

Not so the dream. She had it by the tail just before it slithered back into its hole. Some foreign place where gibberish was spoken, peopled with outlandish faces (a great discovery, so it had seemed, that genes accounted for only minor variations, that in the main human features were molded over a fundamental bone of speech). The search was on for one whose present whereabouts were known to her alone. They tried to make her tell but she refused although she knew the purpose of those instruments on the boil. Torture sanitized. They approached with hot tongs held at the level of her eye. Not tongs, she saw, but calipers agape as if to measure cranial size. On both temples she felt the heat, a small round spot no bigger than a coin—and that was when she woke. Before the real pain started, she always woke.

That she was awake, no pinch was needed to confirm. Every inch of surface tickled with sensation. It felt, she judiciously decided with eyes still closed, like flies crawling over the sweaty flanks of a stabled horse, requiring only shudder of muscle, twitch of skin to dislodge them. She twitched, shuddered, and sat up. No dreamer's where-am-I? on her lips, she recognized at once the motel unit. More expensive than was their custom. She took a moment to appreciate the lavish use of space, the carefully orchestrated color scheme of muted Howard Johnson orange and green.

The wall she stared at was zebra-striped, sunlight winnowed through horizontal blinds, a mene mene tekel of a sign. The time, the time? This was now the familiar awakening, with the familiar prickle of anxiety, what Alan called—Alan! a little jolt as husband's name dropped into slot—her Rip Van Winkle syndrome, the fear of having slept the better part of life away.

Gold watch not on night table. Not lost—she remembered clearly putting it there just before she fell asleep. Nor misplaced, a search of all the little drawers revealed. Stolen then? Worth stealing, at any rate. Bought with the proceeds of a Las Vegas trip when Alan's new blackjack system seemed to work. Report to the police: it had one of those dark inscrutable faces that gave time only under pressure, she had no idea of its value, put down sentimental, it was a present from her husband.

She twisted half-around to scan the dials, knobs, buttons embedded in the headboard, dubbed by Alan Houston Control. Carefully avoiding those that put the bed through its paces, she found the radio, caught a local station in mid-commercial. In time it would announce the time. Meanwhile she had to settle for disco music of faded vintage, more suitable to midnight than a morning sun served up in bright white slices.

Something missing—but of course. To have known, before it could be known, that the watch was gone was indeed remarkable. She was not at all surprised to discover talents, hitherto concealed, that were remarkable. What did surprise her was the watch was gone and she felt no loss. She tried to manufacture a modicum of dismay: alas, alas, a rare gift from Alan, commemorating an even rarer winning streak. Not to speak of affection.

Alan, yes. He had pressed for this vacation, a few days alone without the baby. The baby. The baby. A mother doesn't forget, even for a moment, the name of her baby. Mary mother of God. No, Mary Rowland, *her* mother. Barbara, sister. Josh Greenberg, first boy she ever. Ed and Norma Rabin—next-door neighbors, best of friends, had an old German shepherd, arthritic, Lupa was her name. The baby—

Miranda! Miranda!—loved the dog (Lupa, Lupa), wouldn't miss
mommy and daddy at all, if Norma was to be believed.

Funny, she hadn't thought of Josh for years. Not since out of the blue
his letter came, never answered.

Alan. Miranda. Lupa. Josh. Names rolling about in a pinball
machine, hitting bumpers, flashing lights, TILT, on the score screen an
image appeared. Alan: shaking clenched fist, his mouth with that exas-
perated twist of patience once too often tried even when talking to the
dice. Miranda: tail end of tantrum, eyes restored to limpid blue, gazing
about with equable stare, while from her mouth still issued, like car-
toon balloons, screams of rage. Lupa: dragging haunches, head
abashed, only a dog could feel such guilt for its own chronic pain. And
Josh—

Josh? Were the faces of first loves always so vague? Memory
squinted hard but all it could see was Theseus in opaque panty hose and
some old lady's plumed velvet hat. *A Midsummer Night's Dream,* the
senior play. She was Helena. What a pretext for a camping trip—they
would rehearse each other! No sooner had they doused the fire and
crawled into his sleeping bag than it began to rain. How they had
laughed when it turned out those gustatory sucking sounds were but the
slurping of the mud. Madmen, lunatics, and lovers—all laughers, you
might say. Some rehearsal. She had remembered all his lines, fluffed
her own.

The phone rang. Shrill summons. She felt a sudden trepidation.

"Wally there?" A man's voice, brusque with impatience.

"Sorry?"

"Who is this?" Sharper now, barbed with suspicion.

She shifted hard plastic to other ear, wiped sweaty palm on orange-
flowered sheet. "Sorry?"

"Hey, is this Room 43?"

The key was on the table, where the watch should have been. "No,
this is 44." His turn to say sorry.

"Shit," he said.

Even after the click, she was slow to replace the phone, as if uncer-
tain the conversation was over. Who is this, and all she could say was
sorry. Yet the loss of her name, like the loss of the watch, left her
unperturbed. She knew exactly who she was, it hardly mattered what

she was called. Except, of course, in answering the phone. Who is this? It's on the tip of my tongue, she practiced, don't go away. And while the party waited, she'd run through some vital facts: Mary Rowland is my mother, I have a sister Barbara who is thirty-two, her birthday was last Saturday, my father was Frederic (without a *k*) Rowland, he died of leukemia the day I graduated from college, and I married Alan Whitfield and we have the cutest little baby (Miranda, Miranda, she repeated as if cramming for a test) and as soon as the day-care center has an opening, I'm going back to work. There was no end to the identifying data she could produce upon demand. Like a poet—ah, Josh, she softly laughed, I remember still your lines though not your face—who can give an airy nothing its local habitation; all that's missing is its name.

She took herself in hand. Seriously now, she said aloud, which only made her giggle. Seriously now—this time she kept it firmly to a thought—the thing to do is check your purse. It was hanging over the doorknob, in plain sight, something no thief would overlook. Yet over-looked it must have been—she could feel the wallet, its sole content undisturbed. She withdrew the hundred-dollar bill, bank-crisp, crackled it gaily in the air, all the while doubtful it would pass as legal tender. Easier to cash a personal check, except—no checkbook. And not a single credit card. Wise precaution that filled her now with fool-ish laughter. She slapped hand to mouth—don't laugh aloud when you're alone, nothing sounds crazier—but watery eyes insisted it was very very funny, looking for a credit card to establish your name.

She sat on the bed, dumped out the lot with childish glee. Just as, very little, very young, she would turn mother's purse upside down, shaking all the contents out, then one by one dropping them back in, odd objects of unknown purpose, interesting shapes, what they were did not matter, the whole point of the game the emptying and filling, the taking out, the putting in. If anything, her memory had grown keener, she couldn't have been more than two or three. Unless she had really pulled a Rip Van Winkle, awakening to senility, a sclerosed memory bank with essential data randomly erased, calling up without command the trivia of the past.

Don't stop, baby, don't stop, baby, don't stop, baby, the radio was playing and she became aware that her upper torso was jerking in galvanic response. Once heard, the female voice segueing in and out of the heavy instrumental beat could no longer be ignored. She began to listen for, await expectantly, that lyrical outburst varied only by an occasional sharp shriek. *Don't stop, baby, don't stop, baby, don't stop, baby* . . . . The unmounting tension, the one level of excitation beyond which the music refused to climb, grew steadily more intolerable. Not passion as Tristan and Isolde knew it, not even sex as ground out by the *Bolero,* this was a clinical case of priapus, nerves thrilling to erotic stimulation until, denied their rightful discharge, they fibrillated with exhaustion, sensation passing over from pleasure to pain. The record ended, though the music would not. The fade-out seemed merely to distance it beyond human hearing, a three-note rendition of the agony of desire now rutting in the ether, shaking the cold timbers of outer space.

The voice that followed was deeply masculine, resonant with authority, the voice of a substantial man, affluent yet not without concern for those still struggling up the ladder. *Are you getting the information you need to keep the world in perspective?* She clutched the empty purse, awaiting the mellifluous answer. And was informed that what she sought could be found only in the *Wall Street Journal.*

He was right, the purse proved useless. A small brush, bristling with its catch of tan hair the color of fine dust, came as a shock. She could have sworn that she was gypsy dark, though not until that moment had she questioned the self-image with which she awoke. Aware of the need to relieve more than curiosity, she ran into the bathroom. Ah here was luxury indeed, a separate glass-walled shower stall as well as a sunken tub, and velvet-padded hangers not locked into the rod but left free to filch. As for the mirror she sought, it stretched room-long over an equal length of plastic table top laminated with swirls like marble.

What she saw was a tall foxy blonde who looked as artificially bred as beige mink. She stared long and hard at the face with critical intent. It had the kind of stylishness that could adjust to any momentary trend, that shunned the permanence of character. It was, in short, a face that took no risks. She disowned it.

At least she recognized her things. Every object that belonged to her was clearly labeled hers. Of the two terry robes, raw toweling androgynous in cut, the white was hers, the navy his. The toothbrush with four rows of bristles, hers; the three-rowed version, his. The magazine on the dressing table rolled into a cylinder as if fated to be preserved like a Dead Sea scroll, hers; his the newspaper tossed into the wastebasket.

She heard the outer door open, close, the squeak of bedsprings. Her heart gave an answering squeak as if on it had fallen the weight. Carpeting with the synthetic springiness of astroturf absorbed all sound of her advance. She looked down at a figure of exhaustion, face buried in the crook of the arm. She knew her things.

"Don't tell me," she said. "You lost it all on the last roll."

An affirmative groan. "I let it ride for nine straight passes. Do you know what that came to? If I hadn't crapped out, do you know how much we would have taken home? Over ten grand."

"My God," she said advisedly, identifying the unaccustomed feeling as awe. A moment of silence seemed his due. The crooked arm changed its connotation from warding off the light to warding off a blow.

"Say it." He bared his face. She smiled, finding it a pleasant arrangement of features. She particularly liked the eyes, their warmly hazel frankness, although she recognized all was not as advertised, it was the look he wore when broke, about to cadge a loan. As for the pockmarked cheeks below, one could say their deeply pitted, grainy texture, reminiscent of huge limestone building blocks, added strength. Her fingertips itched to stroke them, already sure of the feel of some hard immutable substance formed over eons, fossil-rich.

"Say what? Okay, you're a better man that I am, Gunga Din. My heart couldn't take it. Ten grand!"

The brow lifted to an incredulous height. "It's a sickness, go ahead, say it, let's get it over with."

She tried to round her eyes into equal frankness. "Why should I say that? I only wish I had your nerve."

Disbelief was all he registered. She sat down on the bed and said emphatically, "My hero!" and when that only seemed to make it worse, leaned over and licked suspicion off his lips like salt. "Do you like that?" she breathed, "and that? and that?"

"Oh, baby," he groaned, "oh baby, oh baby," his fingers plowing through her thick dark hair to clutch at the roots with the convulsive grasp of a man drowning.

They showered and dressed freshly casual for breakfast. "I could eat a horse," he sang out.

"Me too." She had not felt such unambiguous hunger since she was a child awakening to a school's-out June humming of country air. She felt virtuous, as if such appetite were an amazing grace. "Shouldn't you sleep?" she asked with the wifely concern usually reserved for bread-winners. "You were up all night."

But no, he had passed the point of no return, was well into another biorhythmic cycle. "Maybe I'll take a nap before we check out but our last day, we ought to make the most of it."

He must have asked himself how to, when penury barred him from the gaming tables, for he was sad again. To cheer him up, she reasoned victory out of defeat. At least they would not have to reverse the upward mobility of their holiday, from those outhouse cabins of Palm Tree Court to this spacious suite at El Dorado, achieved by means of earlier winnings; they would be homeward bound that afternoon.

"Oh," he said, as if suddenly remembering a message left for her by someone else, "I came back last night and hocked your watch."

My thief, she thought with abstract fondness. "It doesn't matter."

"I trust you have the usual tucked away to get us back home."

Her eyes brimmed with affection as she considered how trust met trust. The hundred-dollar bill still in her wallet—that he had not touched. It struck her as quaintly honorable that he abided by the rules.

"We've a few hours left, you take this, I've got this feeling that your luck has turned."

She enjoyed the way he stared at her, bill in hand, flushed with new hope, but no more flushed than she with the joy of giving all, not holding back.

"You're sure now," he asked, with such fidgety impatience to be off that she laughed.

"I'm sure," she said, but he was gone.

And was back. Eyeing him over her second cup of coffee, so thoughtfully provided by a machine attached to the wall, she could read his fortune even without his lavish gesture of pulling out the linings of empty trouser pockets.

"I'm sorry," she said, and added sugar to the saccharine, no longer worried about calories in excess. "I was just thinking you probably needed a bigger stake."

"You're not yourself, honey." His touch was a diagnostic test—hand on brow—but she was pleased by even such mock concern, by even that shopgirl's endearment.

"Honey yourself," she said and the sweetness of honey was on her tongue. "It was my idea, how could I blame you. I still think it was worth the gamble and besides, there's no use crying over spilt milk." She winced. She should have used another adage than the one her mother chose when told about their marriage. "Miranda!" she said brightly, to change the subject. "The sooner we get home, the better. I miss her, don't you?"

Yes he did, according to his tender smile. "But—I hate to bring this up, my sweet—"

His "my sweet" was always more acidic than his "honey," so she hastened to assure him she knew all that. "Of course we can't head out without some cash. I'll send an SOS, no big deal."

Relieved, he stroked her hair. "I know how you feel about asking your family for anything, believe me, honey, I hate it too, you don't have to sound like you don't mind."

"But I don't." Not a cloud in the sky, he might read in her sunny gaze. "What's a family for, if not to bail you out?" The only question: call her sister, or call her mother? It struck her as particularly fitting when he suggested they toss a coin. Barbara came up heads, as well she should. It was understood by all that Barbara had the brains.

She sat on the bed's edge with the tentativeness of a virgin subject to attack, picked up the phone, and dialed. And heard: Sorry I'm not in just now at the sound of the beep please leave your name the time you called and any message. I'll get back to you as soon as I return.

One little hiccup of panic—leave her name?—but the sound of the beep served as starting gun and she was off! "Guess who," she announced, "I don't know the time, Alan's hocked my watch, but I've got a message." Safely out of the starting gate, she took a deep breath, caught her stride. "You and mom, you always used to say that with my looks, I needn't worry, I'd make out, meaning like it's just as well I've got a face, that's all I've got, but I'm not half so stupid as you think. If you want to know what's stupid, this is what's stupid: here I am, not even thirty, and I've already opened a retirement account. You know what?" She knew what, and more beside. Put on a final burst of speed to cross the finish line. "That boring bank job, I'm never going back." She had said it all but the implacable machine still panted to record. "Bye now," she threw it and hung up.

Alan, small-time gambler, looked glum. "What's that all about? You like that job—it may not pay much, but the hours are good and we need the insurance. I hope you remember we agreed before the baby came I didn't make enough for you to stay home."

She remembered that. Also the Red Cross instructor who, when she was five, took her in a pool and said trust yourself trust yourself and took away his arms and the miracle occurred, she could float. "Who's staying home? Don't you worry, I'll find a job." Or found a business. Dress designer. Tax accountant. Go to law school and argue cases before the International Court of Justice, or into the wilds of Borneo and study orangutans. Speech therapist. Conductor—Amtrak or Philharmonic, either, both. Photographer of royalty and corporation presidents. Newspaper columnist—start off as Dear Abby, work up to Flora Lewis, she felt that buoyant. "There's no end of things I could do."

"Except ask her for money, I presume."

"Shh," she said, dialing again. "I'm calling mother, Barbara wasn't in."

In support, Alan stretched full-length beside her. Through the ringing she could hear her mother's ritual response: now I wonder who that can be. Always as if it were the middle of the night. "Hello, mom," she put her mother's mind to rest immediately, "this is me."

As usual, her mother was amazed, had just been thinking about her, and then the phone rang. Since this happened every time she called, she no longer put much stock in her mother's extrasensory perception, had come to the belief it was an apology of sorts, that her mother never thought about her. And fine, fine was the obligatory response to her mother's opening queries. Fine, fine, she said now and looked down at Alan to share a knowing wink. Poor thing, sound asleep, finally admitting to exhaustion. To forestall what was surely coming next (what's that Alan of yours up to now?—not Alan, a proper noun, but an alan, a species of the animal kingdom, of which the one she owned would win no prizes) she hurled the first thought that bobbed to surface.

"Do you remember Josh, mom?"

"Josh? Josh who?"

"Josh Greenberg, of course you remember, I went out with him in high school. He was valedictorian of our class, remember?"

"Oh yes, that smart Jewish boy. Is he in the news or something? I'm not surprised, I always thought he would make something of himself. Some smart cookie, I remember your father saying."

"Too smart for me, you all made that pretty clear."

"Why whatever makes you say a thing like that?"

An interesting mind, her mother said. One smart cookie, her father agreed. I'm afraid you don't have much in common, her mother said. Just don't get in over your head, her father warned. Barbara hooted: I know that kind, a real make-out artist, you think he likes you for your brains?

"Oh I dunno, I just wanted to tell you I heard from him. After all these years. I was the love of his life, he says. Can he see me again, he wants to know. How about that, huh?"

He says, he wants—she had used the historical present, she quickly decided, she wasn't confused. She remembered exactly when the letter came—one week to the day after father died. Condolences, she had thought, but of course he hadn't heard. The snapshot fell out first. Who is that girl, she had thought. The campfire lit up the face, modeled the cheekbones, hollowed the eyes. A nighttime shot, in black and white, underexposed. The hair looked dark. Wild and kinky was the fashion then, that awful permanent. On the back he had written My Gypsy Bride, but all that proved was how the camera can lie.

"It's always good to hear from childhood friends, dear. You must write him a polite note, making it clear that you are happily married."

"Why mother," she gushed with relish, "I never thought to hear you say so. Better an alan, you mean, than a smart *Jewish* boy."

The mimicry was perfect. She heard the gasp but was not sure if that sharp intake of outraged breath came from her mother or from her. How could it be that she had never heard it that way before? When he received no reply (how could she answer, knowing that fully exposed she was no dark gypsy, just a dumb blonde) was it there he heard the accent fall?

"Now Cissy, is that a nice thing to say?"

Cissy. Strange, she could hear Josh's retch more clearly than the squawking noises emitted by the phone. That full-bodied yuk! of a seventeen-year-old: You mean to tell me it's not short for anything, I've been calling you Sister in baby talk?

"I keep telling you, don't call me Cissy, that's not my name." She slammed down the receiver, the connection was dead. She savored the rage. Champagne of emotions. Uncorked, its effervescence overflowed. She felt a light-headed urge to declaim.

"Who the hell is Barbara to relate the whole world to her?" she roared. Her alan turned over, presenting his back. "Like there's only Barbara and not-Barbara, Barbara and Barbara's sister. Cissy! Yuk!"

That's dumb, Josh said, what's your real name. The only one who ever cared. But she wouldn't tell him, not just then, she was too mad because he called her dumb. Guess, she said.

Guess, she commanded now and tried to frown so that it would look, if anyone were looking, as if she was making a serious effort to recall. But the frown kept sliding off, her skin was stretching, she was yeasty with laughter rising like bread. She leaped up and began to jump around the bed, hopping on one leg, chanting in glee:

> "Today I bake, tomorrow brew,
> The next I'll have the young Queen's child.
> Ha! glad am I that no one knew
> That Rumpelstiltskin I am styled."

From Alan came a groan, a moan, a stir. She flung herself down beside him, snuggled up. "Oh Alan," she giggled, "this is better than pot, do you suppose there was something extra in that joint last night?"

Mmmm, he droned. A hand fell heavily on her hip.

"I know, you just want to sleep. I'll tell you a fairy tale then." She lowered her voice to a bedtime croon, hugged him as if he were Miranda. "Once upon a time there was an evil dwarf—" The crooning stopped. The frown stuck, advising this was serious. *Was* he so evil? Or more so than the rest of that crew? A nasty lot—braggart miller, foolish daughter, greedy king. Upward mobility, that was the thing. For which a woman bargains away her child, then welches on the deal. All the riches of the kingdom? Ha! ha!—her scornful laugh could have been the dwarf's—can you imagine what the king, greedy bastard, would have said to that? Once again, just as when she read it to Miranda, Rumpelstiltskin's answer pierced her heart. Tears in her eyes, she squeezed the body in her arms. "And listen, Alan, to what he says," she cried, as if the telling had never stopped. "*Something alive is dearer to me than all the treasures of the world.* Now I ask you, would someone evil say a thing like that?" Into his ear she breathed again the lovely words. "*Something alive is dearer to me—*"

"Oh cut it out, Joyce," Alan muttered and pulled away.

Once it was spoken, she would know her name, she was counting on that. It would work the way, when someone behind you holds out your coat, you slide in your arms and know without looking, just by the feel, it is yours. Tears stopped, breathing stopped, life was put on hold while she slipped into Joyce.

"Joyce?" Her incredulous whisper evoked only a snore. The certainty came from the answer within: No, this is not my coat.

Someone was laughing. Evil ha-ha's from the dark cavern in which the little man lived. Not her name, the name he called in sleep. Another woman lay in his thoughts, his arms, his dreams.

"For God's sake, stop that noise." He sat up in bed, the scowl deepening as he recalled the exigencies of the moment. "Is your mother going to wire the money?"

Dancing round and round, jumping in glee, hopping on one foot, she shook her head.

"How the hell are we going to get out of here? And what the hell do you think you're doing?"

"Guess!" she said.

At his command, she stopped the crazy laughing, but her smile was yet more evil. He would never guess, and oh the penalty he would pay!

The Zeigarnik Effect

What does a woman want?

—Sigmund Freud

The whole world was what Dale wanted. (This was when she was ten, before she married Howard Renwick and settled for two boys.)

Meanwhile, Dale sucked her thumb.

"A big girl like you?" Dale's father traveled a lot. Whenever he came back from a trip, he was surprised she had not yet stopped.

"Nyah, nyah, Dale is dumb, ten years old and sucks her thumb," was a ditty popular in the neighborhood.

Dale's mother tried foul-tasting stuff that came in bottles. She painted it on Dale's thumb with a little glass rod attached to the stopper. One brand was named *No-No;* another, more exigent, *Stop!*

Dale's father was ready to make a deal. He came from New York. Her mother disapproved, called it pure bribery. She was from Alliance, Ohio, and used the word "pure" a lot. They lived in Chicago, because that was where the "home office" was.

On his next trip to New York, Dale's father took her with him. That was part of the deal. After thirty days, if she was still "clean," he would buy her a globe. Sure that was what she wanted? Dale was sure. She put aside her thumb—poor wan shriveled appendage, the comfort of her life. Had she been Robert Burns, she would have made an ode to it, wee, sleekit, cowerin' tim'rous beastie that it was.

New York took her mind off her travail. She stayed with her grandmother in the Bronx, who asked the usual what grade are you in and what is your favorite subject. At the moment, Dale said (as if she had already learned tempora mutantur and sic transit), I am interested in geography. Especially globes. Then, her grandmother said, I'll take you to the Daily News.

If the SUN were the Size of this GLOBE and Placed Here then Comparatively: the EARTH would be the Size of a Walnut and Located at the Main Entrance to Grand Central Terminal.

If the SUN were the Size of this GLOBE and Placed Here then Comparatively: the MOON would be 1/3 inch in Diameter and Placed at the Main Entrance to Grand Central Terminal.

If the SUN were the Size of this GLOBE and Placed Here then Comparatively: JUPITER, largest Planet of our Solar System, would be the Size of a Pumpkin and Located at Columbus Circle.

Her grandmother had red hair that shot out like the corona of the SUN and wore the same brand of jeans as Dale. She smoked long filter cigarettes by which, in the lighting, fingering, flicking, pointing, extinguishing, she expressed as broad a gamut of emotions as those padded-shouldered stars in old movies on TV. By merely flicking her ashes over the railing into the pit, she indicated that the twelve-foot globe with its aluminum shell cast in two pieces weighing one ton each and joined at the equator had been constructed according to her specifications. Now I ask you, is that or is that not a globe, Dale's grandmother said.

Yes, Dale said, that's a globe.

Dale's father took her next to Boston, where they stayed with her aunt. Her aunt heard that Dale had been taken by her grandmother to see the globe at the Daily News. She took Dale to the Christian Scientist Building. The globe there was so big the people stood inside and saw the world surrounding them. Now *this* is a globe, her aunt said.

When they got back to Chicago, Dale received her reward. It was a penny bank, straight from Woolworth's, with a slit in the North Pole. You can't deny that that's a globe, her father said and winked at her mother.

When you haven't sucked your thumb for thirty days, and then you start sucking it again, it tastes like a stranger's, Dale noted in her diary. It was the last entry she ever made.

> It's friendship, friendship
> Just a perfect blendship
> When other friendships go up in smoke
> Ours will still be oke
> Lahdle-ahdle-ahdle-chuck, chuck, chuck.
>
> —Cole Porter

Dale first encountered Charlotte Puselli at a sandbox. By then, Dale had been a New Yorker for seven years, the wife of Howard Renwick for five, and a mother, sometimes it felt, forever. She had two boys— Stevie, two, and Mark, four. Charlotte had two girls of matching age. It was soon evident they had more in common than their motherhood. They were both Libras, preferred a woman gynecologist, believed in natural grains, opposed nuclear power, liked tennis, hated jogging. Charlotte was eager to resume her career, but thought it better to wait until the younger child entered school. Dale too. Charlotte confided that her husband was of a different faith and that they had yet to decide what to do about the children. "Oh no, it's too much!" Dale cried in disbelief. "The same here, we too!"

Their husbands met and liked each other. Both families joined the Ethical Culture Society. The Renwicks needed a larger apartment, and the Pusellis alerted them to a vacancy in their own building. The friendship grew closer.

There were of course a few small areas of friction. Rent control was one—the Pusellis enjoyed it, the Renwicks did not. Howard Renwick never ceased to smart under the injustice of paying more for less space in the same building. On the other hand, he beat Tony Puselli regularly at squash. They also differed on child-rearing: the Pusellis were permissive, the Renwicks authoritarian. And whereas Charlotte cooked great dishes and sewed terrific clothes for herself and her two girls, Dale maintained a high degree of nonproficiency in all the household arts. As far as sewing went, Dale stapled on buttons, ironed on patches and turned up hems with scotch tape. When a needle was required (as when a boy split a seam), she left it up to Howard, who as a kid had undergone survival training at a summer camp. Okay, that's done, he would say, taking the last stitch, biting off the thread, slapping the boy's behind. Moreover, Howard really liked to cook.

Dale's friends remarked invidiously on her luck. "Now Tony," Charlotte said, lapping up Howard's chili, "is a sexist bastard through and through."

They were on their first—and last—joint camping trip. "Oh, Howard is a sexy bastard too," Dale countered. Charlotte hooted and almost fell in the fire.

A Freudian slip of the ear? Dale looked away from Tony. It had been building up between them like a summer storm—a stillness of breath, a portentousness of touch. Dale swore never to go camping again. What did it amount to, this wilderness bit, but enduring bad weather and each other's children. Bickering with Howard within the moldy confines of a tent. Tony and Charlotte were at it too, Dale could hear. They sat around the campfire, Tony played the guitar. They sang country western and Cole Porter. The kids, except for Stevie, played some kind of game with flashlights. The beams danced like fireflies in the distant dark. Stevie, who didn't like the dark, hugged Howard's knee. Dale nibbled toasted marshmallow from Tony's stick. Howard contemplated the fire. Dale contemplated Tony. Just the thought of Tony as her lover was a lifesaver, like an antidote to swallowing a household detergent.

Nothing happened on that trip. (Another thing Dale had against the wilderness: the lack of privacy.) Dale dismissed the whole idea as a transient atmospheric disturbance. And sure enough, back in the city, the weather changed. They were all very busy, Charlotte back at work from nine to five and Dale with oddly scheduled classes to teach. And besides, Charlotte was her friend. Dale had yet to fail a friend. As it happened, when it happened, it was Con Ed's failure, not hers.

"Who is it?" Dale whispered the night the lights went out, having first double-locked the door. Tony whispered back, as if something had him by the windpipe too. Dale giggled at herself, at him—Pyramus and Thisby with courteous Wall between—and let him in. He had just come to see if there was anything she needed. Charlotte was worried: Howard out of town, poor Dale alone up there with the kids. Dale told him—scolding as one scolds the husband of a friend—he could have used the phone instead of scaring her like that. He had his excuse in hand—a clutch of candles—did she need candles, Charlotte kept a big supply. Plenty of candles, Dale assured him, not to be found wanting, any less prepared. More judicious, perhaps. She thought it dangerous to spot candles about—one never knew with kids. She had one burning only in their bathroom, where nothing could catch fire. "Stevie is the only one who's scared. Remember when we were camping?" They remembered when they were camping. Dale thanked heavens, aloud, that both kids were sound asleep.

The beams from the flashlights pooled at their feet. They moved cautiously as if the hall were land-mined. In the doorway of the living room, he brushed against her. A frisson of passion passed over her skin—the other side of horror, past goosebumps and raised hair. The storm broke then, wreaking its havoc in total silence. They wanted nothing on the record, not even the creak of springs. There was thick carpeting under foot. Under back.

"Mommy. It's so black outside. I'm scared." Standing in the doorway, candle aloft, lacking only a white nightgown and a tire to be the little tyke in that old Firestone ad, stood Stevie.

Later, it was funny, the way they crawled about on all fours, looking for the candle Tony supposedly had dropped. Later, it was a relief, to have been stopped just there, to have never followed through. For later, when Charlotte confided she was thinking of divorce, Dale could say, knowing herself blameless, "Oh, no!"

> Zeigarnik adopted the general procedure of interrupting each task "at the point of maximal contact between the subject and the task.". . . The subjects characteristically showed both a strong resistance to interruption and a decided tendency to resume an interrupted task. . . .
>
> —Crafts et al.
> *Recent Experiments
> in Psychology*

Howard was putting a sharp edge on his cleaver when Dale came into the kitchen on a Tuesday. She had put on a new velour top over her jeans and the eye makeup she never applied before five (an obscure corollary of her mother's rule about drinking hard liquor). Howard asked where the hell she thought she was going.

The Renwicks kept a duty roster in the kitchen. Wednesday and Friday evenings were assigned to Howard. On those nights, Dale had an eight o'clock class to teach and Howard dutifully did the dishes and kept an eye on the boys. Tuesdays and Thursdays were assigned to Dale—these were Howard's free nights, constitutionally guaranteed.

On Tuesdays, Howard had his own class, Chinese Cooking for Beginners. Need he remind her, he reminded his wife, he was due at Mrs. Wu's apartment in less than an hour? Dale reassured him. She was not going out, just upstairs to 16-B. Just for a minute, to take a quick look around. Did he remember the old woman who used to ride the elevator up and down, pushing all the buttons? She had died last week. There was a notice in the lobby that the contents of her apartment were for sale.

Howard looked more alarmed than reassured. He did not share Dale's enthusiasm for buying other people out. The worst junkie was a junk junkie, he had told her more than once and told her now. Dale made the moue of one misjudged. Of one who altruism was established in her genes. She had thought to look for rice bowls, ginger jars, ivory chopsticks—just what Howard would want to have on hand when he cooked Chinese. The Spoffords—hadn't Howard heard?—were old China hands, missionaries from way back, who had fled the Japanese. "The super tells me the place is loaded with stuff they brought back," Dale said, causing Howard to remark on what a cumbersome flight it must have been.

Dale's eyes looked true-blue, the flattering effect of green velour, but Chinoiserie was not what she had in mind. Old women who clung to life as long as Mrs. Spofford had were apt to cling to any kind of junk: old issues of *Cosmopolitan*, out-of-print trashy books, broken strings of lapis lazuli beads, moth-eaten paisley shawls, road maps from a time when cars were called roadsters with familiar affection, like a chuck under the chin. Rice bowls had been a spur-of-the-moment thought to throw Howard off the scent. It worked. Howard even wished her luck.

In the elevator Dale ascended with a resident couple whom she knew by floor, not name. The man was splayfooted. Splayfootedness offended Dale; she saw in it a sign of feckless character. The woman had an ugly monumental head, a small affordable replica of those on

Easter Island. They clucked over "poor Mrs. Spofford." Dale refused to cluck over the demise of a woman who rode the elevator as if it were a spectral Flying Dutchman.

Underneath the sociability Dale recognized a threat. This was a grasping pair, ready to snatch from her some rare find in 16-B, going cheap. The woman challenged her with the hard stare of a bully, pronounced it all a waste of time. In her experience, which she now gladly shared, widows who lived alone for thirty years accumulated a mountain of junk. Dale matched her in unconcern, but before the door of 16-B, her heart leaped. A mountain of junk! Howard's last word of warning—"look, don't buy anything unless we really need it"—missed the point. Who attended such sales to fill a need? She had come to define one. To find not rice bowls but an epiphany (going cheap).

The man who invited them in was wearing a Hawaiian shirt and a well-bred tan. "No coats? Thank God, no place to put them." Beyond him a crush of people moved in and out of the long hallway, in and out of the rooms. The sound-mix of disconnected conversation was like a cocktail party's. "You live in the building, eh? I suppose you knew my aunt? Good to know she had so many neighbors who cared. Come in, come in, look around. I've taped the price on anything that's for sale—what's unmarked is not."

He was now the recipient of that bullying stare. "The sign downstairs said the entire contents—"

"Everything," the man said. His arms, flung wide, included himself. "The few things I'm keeping are just to remember the old lady by."

That meant, the woman said to her husband as they moved on, that anything of value was reserved for a dealer, they should have known. Dale lagged behind to lose them, examined a silk wall hanging (no price tag) in the hall. The apartment was of interest in itself. Dale knew the B line of the building well, Charlotte's was a B apartment, but no present-day B apartment looked like this. French doors of many-paned glass. Dark-wooded dadoes halfway up the walls. Bronze chandeliers with little parchment shades over the circle of lights. There were mahogany bookcases with glass doors that locked—the kind that in her high school library had kept incontaminate Boccaccio, Chaucer, and the unexpurgated *Arabian Nights*. The cases were for sale, but the shelves were bare. Not an encouraging sign.

The living room was too crowded; Dale passed it by. A quick trot down the hall and through the bedrooms confirmed her fears. The junk had been cleaned up, cleared out. Not even hangers in the closet. Empty drawers. Plenty of fine porcelain about and silk scrolls behind glass, but none marked for sale. What remained was heavy, undistinguished furniture, overpriced. A waste of time, as the woman said.

Her own hopes dashed, Dale was reduced to thinking of Howard. She headed for the kitchen to look for rice bowls. The crowd in the living room had thinned out. Dale stopped for a moment in the wide doorway, amused by a room muffled like an old lady afraid of drafts—floor blanketed with orientals, windows swaddled with drapes, sofa with down cushions yeasty as a feather bed. But then she saw at the far end—Dale caught her breath—her heart's desire.

A man in a velour shirt as emerald green as her own faced the window, twirling a large globe. Desire welled up so fresh, so imperative, Dale could not understand how a quarter of a century could pass without its fulfillment. That kind of globe, freestanding, rakishly atilt on its axis, was what she had always wanted. Her thumb twitched with its own bone-deep memory, sent her hand on automatic grope into her pocket. The discovery that she had no cigarettes caused a momentary panic. Howard had found it easy to give them up, was pressuring her to make another try. Five, ten years of extra life, he promised her, but Dale was not one to fall for flimflam twice.

The man stopped twirling, leaned over, showed all the interest of a prospective buyer. Dale addressed a look of fear and loathing at his back. Herself, age ten, surfaced again, ardent practitioner of telepathy, who with eyes squeezed almost shut and mouth compressed and all thought aimed at the back of a head would send out an arbitrary command: *Turn around! Scratch your nose! Tie your shoelaces!* She was doing it now. *Don't buy it!* Straining as at stool. *Don't buy it!* He scratched his nose and turned around.

"Tony." It was more grunt than shout, as if the breath had been knocked out of her. Dale had not seen him since he moved away, leaving Charlotte and the two girls with the apartment downstairs. His hair was shorter. He had lost weight. Looked trimmer, taller.

His surprise was shorter lived. He should have known, he said, he'd find her here.

And did you, Dale's smile asked of him. Did you arrange it all—
taking two years to work it out—knock old Mrs. Spofford off, bring the
nephew over from some island in the Pacific, contrive this neighborly
sale, just to lend an air of serendipity to a meeting obviously fated by
the gods?

Tony held out a formal hand. No, not Tony, evidently. No collusion
there. Dale sent up a small prayer of thanks to those gods whose laps
were so capacious, making specific mention of the eye makeup and
freshly washed hair. Half the pleasure of seeing him was seeing him at
her best. She hadn't changed a bit, he said. Nor he, she lied.

"Frankly, I never expected to see you here," Dale said. Frankly she
was surprised to see him in the building at all, Charlotte made such a
point of keeping him away. The divorce was friendly enough, he saw
the girls whenever he liked but only at his place. "That gives us all a
treat," Charlotte said.

Charlotte and the girls were in California, Tony said. Yes, Dale
knew. They were visiting Charlotte's mother and Disneyland, he said.
Yes, she knew, Dale said, still waiting for him to account for his presence. The cats, he reminded her, the dog. He was the live-in animal
sitter while they were gone. "Poor Hildy, she's grown incontinent in
her old age. I told Charlotte damned if I'd take her to my place, not on
my new carpeting, she doesn't. Nor the cats, for that matter, so long as
she refuses to have them declawed." And how was Howard? And the
boys? Not that he needed to ask about the kids, his girls kept him
posted.

That took care of the kids. And the spouses, present and ex-. Leaving him, leaving her. Warily they circled the globe. There was a price
tag on it. Dale had a momentary shock. Fifty bucks wasn't too much,
was it, she pleaded with Tony, as if she needed a stand-in for a disap-
proving husband. Wouldn't he say that for a globe that size, fifty bucks
was even cheap?

Tony advised against it. As a piece of furniture, it was shot. He
pointed out a crack in the mahogany cradle, a missing ball in one lion-
clawed foot. "It wobbles, see?"

Dale didn't care. The purchase had been made long ago, the price
paid, it was delivery that had been delayed. The Spofford nephew mate-

rialized in their corner. "That's something else, isn't it? Eighteen-inch diameter. You don't see many of those around."

Dale knew she should point out the crack, demonstrate the wobble, offer less, but the very thought of bargaining aroused a superstitious dread. There were rules to the granting of a wish, some understanding exacted by a fairy godmother. Tenuous, fragile, easily reversible. A check passed hands, the globe was hers. Dale looked on it and saw that it was good. The colors of this world were those of childhood's crayons.

"I'll take this down for you," Tony said.

Dale stared deep into the blue Atlantic, concentrated on one thought.

Tony scratched his nose and asked if she had time to stop off first at his—at Charlotte's place for a drink, long time no see and all that.

Dale blinked, released her mouth, relaxed the muscles of her neck. "Yes," she said, then "damn," remembering Howard. She made a quick adjustment in his plan. She would join him later, once she had the boys in bed.

The world was an unwieldly protuberance in an elevator. Tony held open the door by its rubber jaws. Sure she could manage? he asked with a diffidence that had not been there before. He was remembering Howard too, no doubt. Sure, she said, projecting cool competence. She could manage. She would be down in no time at all.

Dale had a well-trained ear. Even before she entered the apartment, she could tell that the screams were coming from the boys' room, from Stevie, not Mark; screams of rage, not pain. Mark had probably hit him, but not hard. From which it could safely be assumed that Howard, tired of waiting, had already left. Howard claimed the kids were old enough to leave alone. Her answer was—and this proved her right— alone yes, but not together.

Dale dumped the globe in a corner of the dining room and headed down the hall. Her step was ominous. Sometimes an ominous step was enough, all would be quiet by the time she reached their room. In the doorway, Dale stared in disbelief. All three of them were there, sprawled on the floor—Mark smirking, Stevie winding down to sniffles, and Howard counting money.

"Monopoly? *Now?*" There was paranoia in her shrill cry. Howard *knew* that Stevie went to pieces when he played that brutal game. Howard *knew* that he was leaving her to put the pieces back again. How could he, she asked first herself, then him. Had he forgotten that he had a class, and already he was late?

Howard apportioned his disgust between wife and younger son. Did she call that a minute? More like an hour.—Why the devil was he crying, just who had asked to play this game?—No thanks to her, but it didn't matter, Mrs. Wu had called to cancel classes for the remainder of the course, her kitchen was burned out, a grease fire started by some private student in the afternoon.—Just because his hotels had been demolished didn't mean that he had lost the game. Remember last time Mark had all his property mortgaged, then came back and won?—What was she looking at him that way for, it was time Stevie learned it wouldn't always go his way.

Howard threw the dice and moved his piece. "Go to jail, go to jail!" Mark crowed. Stevie stole a wad of money from the bank and grew more cheerful. Dale looked on, a woman bludgeoned by the fates, her best-laid plans gone up in smoke. It was still a school night, she finally said. "Mark has homework, Stevie needs a bath, you know how long that damn game takes."

Not to worry, Howard said. This worked on the principle of a floating crap game, they played one hour by the clock, then put everything away as is, to be continued from that point. "That's to get around the cops, you know," Mark said and looked at her with Howard's eyes. Stevie laughed. Dale walked out.

The TV entertained an empty living room. Dale sat in the chair Howard claimed for viewing and envisaged Tony—not the man expecting her downstairs but Charlotte's husband, bringing candles. A movement stopped in a frozen frame. A film device to grab you while the opening credits rolled by.

Howard came in. "Don't scowl," he said. "The game's all cleared away, Stevie's in the tub, Mark's at his desk, and all's right with the world."

Dale didn't buy that. Nor did she respond to the wistful look directed at the chair. Dispossessed, Howard stretched full-length on the sofa. Had she found any rice bowls upstairs, he asked. She shook her head.

He wanted to know why she was watching that crap. She told him to take his shoes off.

Dale had a generous thought. He could still take in a movie, she suggested. Howard had already checked that out. Nothing worth seeing, he said. "Then maybe I will." She reached for the paper, but he beat her to it. He was not about to let her have *his* free night, was the meaning of that grab. Pure dog-in-the-manger, Dale complained.

But Howard could be generous too. Why not go together, if a baby sitter could be found. He scoured the movie ads. There were three possibilities, he said: one about a musician going deaf, one about a dancer going blind, and one about an Olympic skier paralyzed from the neck down. Dale said no thanks, she was depressed enough already.

"Exactly what you need then," Howard said. He recommended highly the you-think-you've-got-problems-well-listen-to-this kind of therapy such a movie would provide. Dale said she had enough of that at home. She doubted that her spirits would be lifted by watching someone else go blind, deaf, and dumb.

"Numb," Howard corrected her and yawned. He guessed then he'd settle for the TV movie that came on at nine, he was too tired for anything else.

Dale looked it up in the TV guide. A crime drama, what else. Far be it from her to criticize his taste, she said, she would say nothing if he really watched those movies, but no sooner did he hear the gunfire and the screeching brakes than he began to snore. It struck her as odd, that's all, to use carnage and mayhem as an over-the-counter, nonprescription drug for sleep.

The FDA would approve, Howard said. It was safe and efficacious.

"And habit-forming." Another listing, same time slot, caught Dale's eye. "Did you know they're rerunning 'Ascent of Man?' " she asked in genuine surprise.

Once was enough, in Howard's opinion. He looked at her and grinned. "But then you had the hots for old Bronowski, as I recall."

Dale ignored the vulgarism. Dear J. Bronowski, she mourned his death afresh. That particular combination of baggy clothes and elegant mind had won her heart. "I wouldn't mind at all seeing it again." She sat up abruptly, inspired by a sudden Keatsian insight. *Beauty is truth,*

truth beauty. All that Howard need know. "That's what I'll do—I'll go down to Charlotte's, no one's using her TV." Or was it the other way around? "They're in California, you know, but I've got the key." And so she had, as Charlotte had hers, mutual insurance against fire and flood and other apartment disasters that had a tendency to strike when the tenant was away. *Truth is beauty, beauty truth*—it sounded right either way.

Howard had no objection, he was glad to have his chair. Dale showed herself solicitous about his comfort. There was cold beer in the refrigerator, she said. He said fine, he'd have some later. She warned him not to touch the leftover chicken, that was for sandwiches tomorrow, Stevie had a field trip. He promised to abstain. His movie had begun. Even before the title and the credits, there was a car chase. "How come there's never any other traffic?" Dale asked critically. Howard was annoyed. What was the matter, he asked, couldn't she tear herself away? Dale felt an obscure resentment. "Oh well, if that's the way you feel about it," she said and left him to his crime.

Her ring of Charlotte's bell set off Hildy's hysterical alarm. "I was just about to give you up," Tony said. The dog's shrill yapping would not stop. Tony's weak commands—"hey, cut it out, stop it, that's enough"—were as ineffectual as Charlotte's. Dale remembered why the camping trip had been so trying: that was exactly the way they handled the girls. The same commands. The same response. "Never mind, it doesn't bother me." The same white lie on her part.

Bored at last, the dog trotted off, flopped under the piano. Dale had not noticed before that Hildy was so old. "It seems like only yesterday Charlotte found her in the park," she said. Fluffy as a powder puff, once that white coat was washed. Now more like a dingy, worn-out mop. "How time does fly, must be a common remark among dogs."

"That, and it seems like only yesterday." Tony jerked her to him. "Now where were we?" He blew the question in her ear.

Dale allowed a moment for recall. "You had just turned out all the lights, I believe." She would have liked to keep their Janus-headed position—he looking over her shoulder (at the future?), she looking over his (at the past?). She was not so sure copulating face to face was the evolutionary advance it was cracked up to be.

Nor was Dale so sure that Charlotte's living room was the right place. Dogs were not the only species to mark their territory. A great cook, a fine sewer, Charlotte, but when it came to the more routine aspects of housekeeping, was oddly lacking. "Forgive the mess," Tony said, as good a way as any to describe it. Nothing like urine on the rugs and cat-scratched sofas with extruded stuffing to make a place look lived in. Dale put her finger on the change in Tony: he looked tightly resewn, newly reupholstered.

Tony turned off the one lit lamp and led her to the couch by hand. Dale felt she was about to be introduced to an invisible presence. "Will that do?" he asked. "Or do you require a fifty-mile radius of darkness?"

Their kiss was a dry recapitulation. Dale reached up to clamp his head. Suddenly between them was the squirming body of the dog, barking, yipping, yelping, whimpering—all of which gave way to noisy slurping, a wet lapping of the tongue. Dale spit dog hair out of her mouth. "What's the matter with her, has she gone completely crackers?" She covered her face with her hands. The tongue found the crevices between her fingers. There was no escaping the fetid breath of old age.

"You little bitch, you," Tony said. Dale bridled although the tone was loving. Then blushed. He was talking to the dog. "She's jealous, that's the trouble. Charlotte used to say that I—"

Dale did not want to hear what Charlotte used to say. She announced she would not fight over any man—certainly not with a dog. Then made an ambiguous sound, half laugh and half allergic snort, at what sounded like a porno movie plot. She plucked Hildy off her chest and held her head back to avoid that tongue expressing so much hostility in the guise of so much love. She had not known dogs were so human, she said.

The only solution, Tony said, was to lock her up. He left the room with Hildy close at heel. By now, Dale figured, Bronowski was asquat on the shore of Samos, proving the Pythagorean theorem. She unbuckled her belt, wriggled out of her jeans. She heard Tony close the door at the end of the hall, just as she and Howard closed off the boys before making love. His returning shadow, cast by the hall light, outpaced him in eagerness, an expectancy larger than life.

He stumbled on her nakedness unprepared, gave a sharp audible

intake of breath, as if he had stubbed his toe. Too presumptuous? Dale
asked, still mentally clocking "The Ascent of Man." Not at all, he said
and crossed his arms in a self-hug, pulled off his shirt. And the telephone rang.

Tony made no move to answer. His unzipping was an act of defiance.
Of the same mind, Dale held out her arms. The caller was stubborn,
the phone kept ringing. As if he *knew* someone was home. "Oh God,"
Dale groaned prematurely. She had just remembered Howard.

A quick conference was called. Howard thought of her here alone,
would surely grow alarmed, it might be wiser to spare him that concern. Tony agreed in disgust to let her rise. But he matched his step
with hers, as if already they were one, took a stand behind her, held her
by the waist as she picked up the phone, keeping his claim in while she
talked to Howard.

For of course it was Howard. Calling, it seemed, to ask how was
lover boy—as good this time as the last? Behind her, Dale felt a sudden
diminution in Tony's interest. Her own heart missed a beat before she
recognized the reference to Bronowski. "Better," she said firmly.

Howard said hell, then it was not the cable it was their set. He could
have sworn it was the cable. "It's been acting up lately, cutting out,
then coming back in." But then if Charlotte's set was working—

Dale found his reasoning laborious. She grew impatient, pointed out
that she was missing the best part. Howard's voice snapped to attention.
"Right, I won't keep you. Tell you what, the kids are asleep, I'll come
down and join you."

Tony gripped her shoulder. "Did I hear—?"

"You heard," Dale said.

They sprinted back, sorted out, pulled on, shrugged into their scat-
tered items of dress. Dale began to laugh, seeing in their hip-grinding,
arm-flailing exertion the low humor of a potato-sack race. Tony
laughed too. He was having trouble getting into his shirt. Winner of the
race, Dale turned on the TV. No picture, no sound. Nothing but snow
and an exasperating drone. She switched channels wildly, cried out for
help. It was the cable. She should have thought, but she had said, and
Howard was coming down. Tony pushed her away as if she were inept
at turning a dial. She eyed his back coldly. He was fiddling while her

marriage burned. She urged him to attend, stop fooling around, they had to get together on a story.

The sound came on. A blast of studio laughter. Then the picture—Merv Griffin's smile, like slightly melted American cheese. Tony turned down the volume, triumphant. The great fixer. What channel, he asked. She told him. Tony objected that it was a rerun—once was enough, he said—but one look at her expression and he obeyed. Bronowski's face was summoned like a genie to the screen. A civilized voice filled the room. "Zip up your pants," Dale said, as they heard the expected ring.

Tony came to a halt, looking foolish. Not the door, the phone. He cocked an ear, like some nature-lover trying to identify a bird call. It might be, Dale agreed. She picked up the phone with the care of a snake-handler working with a specimen not yet defanged. Tony remained fixed to the spot as if waiting to hear "Simple Simon says."

Dale replaced the instrument gently. Relax, she said. False alarm, the TV upstairs was working too, Howard was not coming down. "Just as well," Tony said with a peculiar look. He did not look relaxed, he looked—peculiar. Like Mark or Stevie in last year's clothes. She needed no mirror to know how she must look. The gods, Dale thought, were working overtime. Were they trying to tell her something? They should have asked her mother. That girl, her mother would have told them, is pure stubbornness, you can't tell her anything.

"I think that's *my* shirt, sir," Dale said. Her voice was shaky.

"And I think that's mine."

Laughter was inadequate. They tottered, fell upon each other. "Careful," Dale moaned, "that's *my* armhole you're tearing. I think we'd better make a swap."

"Let me help you," Tony said.

But he turned out to be the one who needed help. The trouble was, Dale could have told him had she been willing to admit to trouble, nothing so demeaned high passion as low farce.

Okay, that's done. Howard taking the last stitch, biting off the thread. Dale shivered. What was Howard's voice doing in her head?

"Good for you too, hmmm?" Tony murmured, smiling at the ceiling, eyes still closed.

"Hmmm," Dale agreed. She looked at her watch. "The Ascent of Man" was over. "Dale," Tony began when she reached for her jeans. She put her finger to her lips, then to his, signing a kiss, signing shut up. Propped on his elbow, he watched her dress. When she was ready to leave, he tried again. "Dale—" She pinned him back with an ineffable smile. "Don't say it," she said.

Dale closed her own door quietly. The rising swell of music announced the movie's end. She had no doubt that Howard was asleep.

"Dale?" His voice pounced on her from the rear. He was in the dining room. "Come in here." The command had a minatory ring. She obeyed. The sight of the globe shocked her. She had forgotten all about it. Howard waited until she stood beside him, sharing his view of the blue Pacific. "How much did you pay for this?"

Dale looked at Howard's face and lied.

"For this piece of junk?"

He gave the globe a disgusted twirl. She slipped her foot under the damaged claw to keep it steady. "Look." He stabbed with a finger. "Cochin China. Cochin China, by God. And the British Empire, on which the sun never sets. All that red. And there's Africa for you—the brown is German, the purple French, more British red of course, and yellow is—" he leaned over, peered at closer range—"Portuguese. Do you realize how out of date this is?"

Dale looked properly sheepish. The crack could be repaired. A new ball under foot would end the wobble. But how could she not have noticed that the world itself had changed and nothing could fix that.

The Perfume of Love

Keys forgotten again, she had to ring for Mike to let her in. Cursed February and its bitter wind. Cursed the down coat, so unmanageable at the meeting, billowing over adjacent seats, having to be hauled in like a hot-air balloon, unflattering too, making her look like an enormous caterpillar, but guaranteed impenetrable even by an arctic wind, so why did she feel, stabbing her in the back, a cold steel knife right between the shoulder blades? Rang again, cursed Mike for taking so long, never mind she could hear him galloping down the hall to make amends.

He opened to her, sly with delight, as if it were her birthday, a surprise party inside, causing her to suffer a momentary vertigo of doubt: Could it be for some such noble purpose, not base comfort, that he had welched on his promise to attend the meeting? Come get your valentines, the chairman had called out, waving a stack of petition forms; otherwise she would not have marked the date.

"Theresa's coming home, I was just on the phone." Exigent in his gladness, Mike waited for a mother's cry of joy. Settled for an ambiguous noise, which could have been a cluck of pleasure or, within the subtext of that red nose, the tail-end sniffle of a crying jag. "You look frozen stiff." He refrained from comment on the new button she was sporting. *Freeze Now,* it read. His restraint was wasted. Squeezing past him, Adele did not acknowledge his existence, much less the superior judgment he had displayed in staying home.

He stood ready to help her out of her coat—those good manners that her friends admired—but Adele was sure, from the clamminess of the hall, he had fudged the thermostat still lower while she was gone. The recent oil glut had not diminished in the least his concern at wasted energy. She called it crazy. Any fool could see the danger was the world would end in fire, not ice. She pulled off her wool cap to uncage wild crackling hair, but said no thank you she would keep on the coat, and to make her point did so until upstairs. The bedroom was, as he promised, somewhat warmer but not so warm she wouldn't need a flannel robe. She zipped it up with a violent pull, more a tearing than a closing.

"I suppose I'd better call the office in the morning, stay home."

"I was just thinking that. It doesn't seem right to leave her to an empty house her first day home." Suddenly she looked tired to him. He came up from behind, pinioned her before the mirror. "Frankly, my dear—"

Against her will, she laughed at the mugging he was doing over her shoulder. Was more angry, not less, for having laughed. "We should never have gone to that damn movie last night. Better to have stayed in bed."

Neither had seen it since it first came out (for her a landmark of sorts, when Clark Gable broke down that bedroom door: the first time she had felt pure pulp and jelly, the literalness of thrill). And I thought that racist garbage the greatest movie ever made? Mike had cried, appalled. That boxer's face chewing its cud—to *that* she had thrilled? They figured it out—he was fifteen when it was made, she was twelve—and felt a little better.

"What I was going to say is a day off will do you good. You could use the rest." But he was still looking in the mirror.

"Oh work on those dimples by yourself," she said and squirmed free.

She went into the bathroom, came out. Mike was completely unprepared for her explosion.

"Why couldn't she come at Christmas, when Micky was here, when she hasn't seen her sister in five years, and she's never seen the twins, and I was off on vacation?"

"Look," Mike said and Adele gritted her teeth. He was going to be rational. "You're mad at me because I wouldn't freeze my ass off and go with you tonight. Well say so, don't take it out on the poor kid. The last thing she needs."

Adele cursed the day she stopped smoking, thinking: I really need one now. "So what is it this time, did she say?"

"There you go again, assuming the worst. I asked her how were things, she said just fine."

Her look told him what she thought of that disingenuous ploy. "Theresa comes home, she's in trouble." She was stating a law.

Mike shifted to stronger ground. "We should consider ourselves lucky. Most kids don't confide in their parents." Sobered by such good fortune, he frowned. His frown—to ward off envy of the gods—moved upward on the bias, thick pleats of forehead skin that reached a terminal moraine at the sharp line where baldness began and the skin stretched tight as a drum. The thought of his girls back home—Theresa especially, since she doled herself out like some expensive morsel affordable only in small tastes—flushed him with pleasure.

"Kids," Adele mocked. Theresa was thirty-one. Had been on her own for eleven years, not counting the occasional relapse when she came home to make veiled allusions to suicide and to pig out— Theresa's words, not hers—on all the dishes she had loved when six years old. "When?" she asked, and was not at all surprised that arrival time was 3:00 A.M. Her "tonight?" was hardly a question, Theresa never gave more warning. Of course Mike would quibble that to be exact it would be tomorrow morning. "I do wish she wouldn't super-save at your expense. You *are* picking her up, I suppose?"

"Don't worry, I've set my watch alarm, you won't hear a thing."

"Oh yes I will. I hate that sound. You know what it's like? Tinker Belle trying to get the attention of Peter Pan. I want you to know I was never one of her admirers. My father took me to that show, I must have been the only kid who didn't clap to save her. Not even when he said damn you, clap, and shook me." She gave Mike the first smile of the evening. "That's neither here nor there, it's you I'm thinking of, you'll be knocked out in the morning."

Mike saw this was a war game. Shuttlecock, not chess. Batting back and forth considerate attentions over a net of hostility. Of her raising, not his. He preferred the *Nuclear Times,* picked it up again from the

stack of doomsday journals to which Adele subscribed, reclined syba-
ritically on the wicker chaise. Best seat in the house for reading,
but one he rarely occupied. Let Adele approach, book in hand, and he
had to remember his manners. Thank you, dear, she always said, and
took it.

The wicker creaked as he adjusted his position. It was hard to read
with Adele so quiet. He kept looking up to check what she was doing.
Watched her assuage chapped face with white dollops of cream, her
eyes fixed on some vanishing point beyond the glass. If she did not
regard her reflection, he did, used it as a mirror of his own decline.
Hers was the kind of face—long and sallow, ravager's eyes, nose a
cutting edge of bone—that age did not change so much as slyly carica-
ture. How much so he had not realized until Micky, home at Christmas, brought back the original version. To that one he had contributed
nothing but his name (luckier the second time around). Michaela made
a lovely sound and its beauty custom had not staled—no one ever used
it. Theresa now—Theresa was a different story.

He turned the page. *Can America Survive the Trident II.* He had to
smile, just thinking of Theresa. Not a child to be shortchanged, even in
the calling of her name.

Without turning around, Adele rebuked his image. "I must have
missed that part—maybe you can tell me just what's so funny."

"What? Oh, in this? Nothing." He put away the journal, removed his
glasses. "I guess my mind was wandering."

Under her breath, Adele bet she knew where to. Theresa, of course.
Who came home only when in trouble. To eat her head off, sleep all
day, and reject any good advice with oh leave me alone. Tell me, Adele
thought to plead, tell me what's so funny about Theresa. But halfway in
her throat the plea became a shout. Denied an exit, it reverberated
inside, shaking her with such force she had to grip the chest.

"What's the matter?" Mike asked. The way she was standing there.
Like a woman going into labor.

"Nothing," she said, and went back to rubbing in the cream. Sooth-
ing strokes on forehead, cheeks, chin, extended throat. The calming
application of the master's hand on a bristling beast. Finally she took
off her watch, shed her rings, adding to keys and loose change—Mike's
little pile—already in the lacquered tray. Each night they joined their

valuables together on the chest which, by virtue of the mirror hung above, served as dresser. But on this the cleaning woman's day, the tray was centered so precisely the whole arrangement smacked of a votary offering to expectant glass. "That woman!" she cried and Mike knew—although the violence of the epithet might more conventionally have been applied to a rival for his affections—just whom she meant.

"What's she done now?" He employed the consoling tone he had developed as referee in arguments between the girls. Adele could never handle them. She found it onerous, dispensing justice—poor Adele, how hard she tried to be fair, when all they wanted, being girls, was someone to take their side.

"Oh you." The "you" of dismissal a woman addresses only to a man. "You never notice anything." Her scorn embraced the whole sex, a barely sensate form of life. Noticed nothing. Not even the deadly symmetry, the last stages of universal entropy, in which once a week this house reposed. Not a chair but faced its mate, coasters dismantled from the stack and dealt out like a deck of cards, four place mats on the dining table because it had four sides, never mind that only two now dined. Even in the kitchen each counter had its centerpiece, here the bananas, there the toaster, and there the leftover morning coffee glowering in its glass pot. She took up her brush, so neatly paired with its comb, and gave grey hair forty whacks in a Lizzie Borden rage. Electrified, it stood out in horror.

She could no more connect her reflection with herself than a dog or cat could acknowledge its, but she still could see her husband. And recognize—therein lay the horror—that the pattern of his baldness had turned out to be exactly like her father's.

It's quiet out there, he mouthed, too quiet, the natives are restless. That was the game they played when more favorably disposed: whole movie plots condensed into one-liners. She passed him without a word to open the window from the top before getting into bed. He deplored that madness of a fresh-air fiend, but the black mood she was in, better not to argue. Almost viscous in its flow, the cold air formed a separate and distinct current, an icy river in a warm sea. The waste of energy smote him in the heart.

Only his shoes kicked off, otherwise fully dressed in readiness for the early rising, he occupied his side of the bed, not deigning to get between the sheets, with only the comforter to warm him, so that they lay antiseptically packaged from each other's touch. The silence was a test of endurance, a kind of arm wrestling, to see who would buckle first. He became obsessed with the sound of her breathing. In and out, he followed the rhythm, and once, when it changed, a longer-than-usual caesura between the out and in, his heart stopped.

"Tapioca."

He must have drifted off. He wasn't sure what he had heard, sure only that she had spoken first. "What's that, dear?"

"Remind me to buy some tapioca, she'll want that. Good thing they print the recipe on the box, I keep forgetting how." Her voice trailed off with a list growing ever fainter. Milk . . . eggs . . . vanilla . . . .

Dredged up from the deep, stranded, beached, flopping on the sheets, he heard a little strangling snort, knew that she at least had floated free. Closed eyes tight, trying even that mimetic magic, but instead of sleep came Theresa. Little girl cooking in the kitchen. He thought cooking because he smelled dessert. But the oven was cold, the counters bare, no mess in the sink. Yet there was the extract in her hand, stoppered by her finger, which she removed to flourish under his nose. At his puzzlement, she laughed. (Not so little either, big girl by then. No more high-pitched giggle, full female crow. And beneath the spartan sweat shirt, the frank luxury of breasts.) You know what I have here? she challenged him. Vanilla? he asked, suddenly not sure of anything. She shook her head. It's perfume, she said. The perfume of love, she said. And—still his baby, still teasing daddy—she raised her arms in the classic pose of womanhood, lifting the weight of all that shining hair, to dab behind each ear the rich brown stain.

2

Down the stairs in stockinged feet, slept-in pants of just the right bagginess, here comes Mack Sennett clown, classic comic of one-reelers, husband sneaking out, night on the town. Mike laughs, a before-the-days-of-sound laugh at spouse deceived: Adele asleep, one arm flung across his vacated place, a standard planted to claim this new land for the queen.

On bottom step he slips on shoes, remembers he has left her thinking Theresa comes as usual by plane. Habit takes him to console table. Must leave last known whereabouts. Just in case is how Adele justifies the rule, but Mike suspects she has kept herself prepared all these years for some hard questioning by the police. She claims he notices nothing in the house but he hates this table—a semicircle of black marble, bracketed to the wall, jutting out like a Ubangi underlip. Union Station, he jots down. Again the lineaments of a laugh stretch his face. It occurs to him he is acting sadly out of character—what husband sneaking out for a night on the town leaves behind an itinerary?

Exempt from wifely admonitions against speeding, relishing the surreal emptiness of predawn streets, he is off on a teenager's driving spree, rattling over potholes, jumping lights, turning with an operatic screech into the once grand plaza of the railroad station. As if inspired by the old car's agility, he takes at a run the great sweep of granite steps, disjointed now with temporary ramps, crude wooden planks laid down for the handicapped. The main waiting room—that magnificent high-vaulted space, expansive as the century which saw it built—is blocked off. Everywhere the turmoil of reconstruction. He is routed into a constrictive passageway with makeshift walls of old wood salvaged from homelier demolitions, mainly doors of different heights, different colors, different panelling. Doors to different lives. A domestic madness that belongs to dreams.

In time to watch the train pull in, he suffers its terminal crawl, final shudder. The shudder is transmitted as by a law of physics to the small crowd shouldering him. A surge forward as the gate is opened, but Mike holds his ground by the cold iron's scissored folds. Not for him a mad rush up and down the platform, peering into cars. No other exit she can take and besides, his long vision is still good.

He keeps a watch on those descending—a motley crew, mostly old, mostly black, mostly poor. Like bombed-out refugees, whole wardrobes layered on their backs, clutching whatever they have salvaged and a crying kid or two. This station calls for gentlemen in chesterfields and felt fedoras, tall ladies in furs, for redcaps trundling wardrobe trunks and pigskin cases, sturdy stuff patinated with exotic ship and hotel labels. Now, he sees, it's mostly shopping bags. And for the heavy-laden, appropriately enough, shopping carts.

He is playing the amused observer to deny a growing panic that he may not recognize his own daughter. So many Theresas have come and gone, they are montaged in his memory like the aliases of a Wanted poster. What are women's changing fashions but a series of disguises? Last seen in long flouncy skirt, cavalry boots, a shako of frizzled curls.

From quite a distance he admires the high-heeled bounce. It takes high heels to show off a woman's ankles. Theresa? In high heels? In high heels, by God. And a high-fashion coat, hanging loose. And under that, what Adele has always called a business suit. Oh daddy, she cries with the same old neck-hug. His muscles tighten in confused reflex, as if expecting to be called on to lift a dangling weight. She smells expensive.

Baby, he says and wonders where that came from. She doesn't seem to mind. But Micky does—or so Adele has always claimed: You never call *her* baby, you think she doesn't notice? The thought of Micky is as distracting as a floater in the eye—the child who never was a child, only a smaller version of her mother, outfitted from the start with Adele's dark elegance of form, like an Elizabethan tot in ruff and stomacher. Not a child you call baby. More to the point, Micky never throws her arms around his neck; she is always holding something. Packages in fancy wrappings of things never wanted, things that never fit. Thank God—he squeezes hard—Theresa never brings them gifts.

You'll crack my ribs, she scolds him. Continues with the scolding: you shouldn't have come, not at this hour, I told you on the phone I would take a cab. Then gives his arm a squeeze to show she doesn't mean it. He tishes and pshaws, discounts any trouble. Something puzzles him about this Theresa. He decides it must be the hair that makes her look so different, women can do that just with hair. He's glad it is straight again, he never liked it kinky. Cut short, a little jagged, smooth calyx for a flower of a face. Suddenly he is terrified, seeing for the first time how it will age, repeating the same mistakes his face has made. Baby, he says, and blinks away the future, picks up her bag. A real one; he appreciates the leather.

Theresa's damn, damn, damn! brings him to a stop. She is glaring at the barricades. Refuses to believe—don't tell me! she commands—that entrance to the station is denied her. Quivering flesh, shoulders raised to accommodate the pent-up breath. That famous temper. Mike still boasts of it as he would of the athletic prowess of a son. Watch it now, he warns her, or you'll get the old one-two. He tries to growl it as a threat, but his tongue is furred with fondness and his face abloom, like a neglected plant rewatered. It takes an effort to suppress a laugh.

He is laughing at Adele, who tried reason. Of course it failed. Terrified Adele, swearing: the little devil, she knows exactly what she's doing when she holds her breath like that! Of course she did. Even turning blue, a calculating eye. There was a horse like that back on his uncle's farm, just you try to saddle it, swelled its belly up with air, and all the while those eyes rolled back, to size you up, to see who was the cannier. Little devil, that's for sure, but he knew how to handle her. Put up your dukes, he'd say and get down on his knees, providing a broad target with his torso for her pummeling. (Ah, such furious joy!—he relishes even now those blows.) Once he cried uncle—it never failed—she turned sweet as pie.

She gives him a token smile, he sees he has annoyed her. Oh you, she says with a flick of a head that has not forgotten when its hair was long. He shrivels a bit at having to relinquish part-claim to this daughter: the looks are his, but the voice Adele's. He hates to admit it but on the phone they're hard to tell apart.

Another squeeze of his arm—again she doesn't mean it—it's just that it's painful to see them do that to a work of art. He looks at the scaffolding, the heavy canvas over gaping holes. Somehow he feels she is accusing him. Of what, he wonders in all innocence. Of a conspiracy of silence, her next words enlighten him—not telling her they planned to tear it down, leaving her to read about it in the dentist's office, a two-page spread in some old magazine.

Honest to God, she swears, if you had asked me I would have said it was the Pantheon (the one in Rome, she is careful to add) and I thought what a shame, here we have this marvelous building, a real temple, and I've never seen it, except passing by in a car, so I figured what the hell, I'd take the train, I wouldn't mind just once arriving in grand style.

He says nothing, not sure he understands her bitter look. She treats him to her heaviest scorn: They couldn't wait, could they, to pull it down, how could they be such philistines?

Philistines? Pulling temples down? To his Presbyterian ears, that sounds wrong. You've got it wrong, he tells her and tries to move her on.

Theresa will not be budged. Looks ready to hurl herself on the barricades. Such intensity of gaze draws Mike's attention. Through those monumental arches, streams of passengers once flowed—he among them. Always, it seems, in uniform: sailor-suited, holding mother's hand; Boy Scout off to camp in official green and hot damn, hooked to belt, official Boy Scout knife; then the real thing, khaki, and in breast pocket the orders for Fort Dix that meant he was shipping out, the exhilaration of a certain kind of terror.

He was lucky, he quickly tells himself, for him there was the coming back. There he was, hardly more than twenty, but with ribbons on his chest to tell you where he'd been and a war packed on his shoulder. And this strange girl meets him. Dad pumped his arm, Mom cried and hugged, no one thought to introduce them. I'm Adele, she had to say herself. His mother's goddaughter, all the way from California, her first visit. Not what you called pretty. The lean and hungry look has never been a wartime style; jacking off at pin-ups of big-breasted blondes gave you a different aesthetic. And yet he hoists the duffel bag back on his shoulder and takes it as his fate that he will love her.

Suddenly Mike feels a horror at these retentive stones, it is like looking at the imprint of a youth long since atomized in a Hiroshima-flash. He wishes they had torn the station down.

Theresa jiggles him, demands how could they, issues her own judgment. They ought to be shot.

Over the wood palings, the tops of the arches peer like raised eyebrows: What? *You* still here? Frankly my dear, is his answer, I don't give a damn. The swagger is pretty good, she recognizes Gable. Punches him with her fist playfully. Oh you, she says, telling him, undeserving as he is, she still loves him.

He leads her through the construction maze, talking a mile a minute (Theresa in high heels makes him strangely shy), telling her just how she's got it wrong. (To catch her expression, he has to redirect his sideways glance two inches higher—it gives him a kind of jolt, as if he has misjudged a step.) They're not tearing down the station after all, he says. A last-minute reprieve, not exactly a full pardon—he wants to be precise—more like a parole. The old station had its problems, maybe she didn't realize: dearth of passengers, too costly to heat—there he could sympathize—and worst of all, it was attracting all the scum, poor devils with no other place to sleep. He prods her memory of the old home town: that crappy Hopedale section, *you* know, all those packing plants. That's the site they've chosen for the new station, which is to be a modern work of concrete art. In other words, another packing shed.

But that's five miles out of town, she objects. That far out, they figure to discourage the bums and drifters, he explains. Passengers too, she retorts. Poor baby, she doesn't seem to realize that passengers are held in the same contempt. But shoppers aren't. He paints a glowing picture of the whole neighborhood upgraded, all this wasted space converted to an indoor mall of specialty boutiques and food emporiums winding around the obligatory jungle core.

Oh well, she shrugs, and supposes that is the usual fate of any pantheon. The structure is allowed to stand, it's the gods they change.

In the middle of the plaza, that funnel for cold wind, she pulls at his duffel coat, makes him stop to admire the classic columns, the Gothic shadows. He tries again to impart the facts of life: this is the kind of place to keep a wary eye on shadows, it is dangerous if they move. But when has this girl ever shown respect for facts? Just imagine walking up those steps to begin a journey, she exhorts him. She compares this ceremonial approach to the convection belts of airports—talk about packing sheds! It must have struck her that he knows those olden times firsthand, for she suddenly demands: didn't it make you feel you were really going somewhere, somewhere different, somewhere that would change your life? He remembers the khaki. It sure did, he says.

Even buckled in—he insists on that—she squirms around to keep the moonstruck dome in sight. At last she settles back. The ride down was lousy, she says abruptly. He is surprised, the train made good time, but it seems she was expecting something different. Like in those old movies, she tries to explain—you know, dining cars with white tablecloths and black porters to put up your luggage with those big smiles. Her sigh abandons hope of ever knowing such courtesies. That snack bar, God, she groans, and turns on the radio. He keeps it tuned to an all-news station and she lets it stay.

So brief a visit, already over? You haven't asked about your mother or your sister, he reproves her. Dutifully she asks. They're fine, he says. And then—he will do anything to please her—he mentions there may be trouble brewing in Micky's marriage. Roger didn't come along on this last Christmas visit, Micky thinks he's seeing someone. Infidelity, he says wonderingly, is Micky's sticking point. Too late he remembers he is not supposed to tell. His own hurt he keeps secret, that Micky told him nothing, confided only in Adele.

I know all that, Theresa says, mother wrote me.

So much for secrets. Nor is there any relish in her tone, she seems to prefer listening to the radio. It occurs to him the subject may have struck too close to home. If he is to give credence to Adele's suspicions, Theresa's latest lover is a married man. (For a moment he is distracted, he cannot think of his daughter's lovers without admiring his own dispassion, and he passes by the one-way street on which he should have turned.) *Really* married, Adele would have him understand, although how she knows she cannot say. You'll see, is all she says. Adele at her most sibylline. No evidence at all, just a wholesome knack for foretelling disaster. But what if she is right, he asks himself and turns into a dead-end street. Backing up, he finds some comfort in divorce statistics. No one's *really* married anymore.

Cheerfully he announces he will have to make a U-turn under the expressway to come back in. Theresa giggles: where's all the time she thought to save coming in by train, avoiding the long drive from the airport? Mike doesn't care how long it takes to get home, now is the part of her visit he enjoys the most, the picking her up on her arrival, the driving her back on her departure. In between is the hairy part, at times like that a girl needs her mother.

True intimacy needs no words, Mike hopes. Into the silence seep hockey scores, an earthquake in Peru, a science report on the diving mechanism of Antarctic seals—or so it seems at first. Mike reaches across, turns it off. Why did you do that, Theresa complains, they think they've found the cause of crib deaths, didn't you hear? She thinks—so does Micky, so does Adele—the family has a vested interest in the subject. How many children do you have? Adele still counts her children beginning with the boy, but Mike correctly answers two, two lovely girls, just two.

If only Theresa would let it go. That was interesting about the seals, she says, I never knew that stuff about a reflex closing off their airway when they go under so they won't drown, and that you find it in the human fetus too. Do you suppose (awe and wonder in her voice) it's like they say, it's that kind of diving reflex left over from the womb that closes down a newborn's breathing—now *that* is fascinating, she says. He hears the pugnacious note on which she ends, daring him to deny her right to remember her own brother. Pretty fascinating, he says to shut her up. Particularly when the baby dives and doesn't come back up.

New job? he asks to provoke just that indignation. You always *assume,* she protests. As a matter of fact, she's now in banking. He laughs out loud. So grandiose a job description. His favorite remains expediter for a restaurant chain, covering her brief tenure as short-order cook. Now why, he wonders, did she give up the job she seemed best fitted for—teaching college graduates how to compose, if that's the word, impressive resumes.

Too bad that tellers are no longer caged, he jokes, or Micky might claim her direst prophecy had come true, Theresa behind bars at last.

But this time she's not kidding, she vaunts that title in all serious-ness. Assistant branch manager is just an entry level job—she gives a modest shrug—she had expected something better from a M.B.A, and to tell the truth, she wouldn't have taken it without the pro-mise that advancement would be rapid. It is the modest shrug that takes his breath away. To tell the truth, she doesn't even have a bachelor's degree.

He would have thought banks were more careful (he sounds a little worried) but no—he shuts her up—please don't tell him how she swung it.

She apologizes. She keeps forgetting—now she laughs at him—her father is a member of the bar.

The trouble is, Mike thinks, they were taught a different grade-school history. Not for them George Washington and the cherry tree. For them—he eyes his daughter, leaning against the window half-asleep—the first president was Nixon, they grew up on Watergate. For a moment he is pleased to have traced the trouble to its source, then remembers Micky, who doesn't fit, who plays by all the good old rules, even stricter than her parents. He gives a head-shake of incomprehension. Who in this day and age demands fidelity?

Gently he touches Theresa: wake up, we're home. It doesn't seem so long ago he would have carried her in, dumped her in the lower bunk, letting Micky, of the sturdy legs, climb up on her own. She wasn't asleep, Theresa grumbles. The whole block looks spruced up, she has noticed, and he's put up new shutters. While he checks the car to make sure all doors are locked, she stares up at the bedroom windows as if admiring the improvement.

Nobody believes me when I say you've had the same house all your life, she says, then giggles. Not to speak of the same wife.

The smartest thing I ever did, he says. He means the house. Moving in when his father died, instead of selling as everyone advised. It was supposed to be worth your life to live here then, smack in the middle of the city—there is something like nostalgia in his voice. You wouldn't believe what I could get for this property today, he boasts. He grasps the wrought-iron railing on the stoop. I fixed this too, he says and shows her it no longer jiggles.

She puts her hand out to test it for herself. So how come daddy— the question erases all he just said—how come you've got such a crazy mixed-up kid?

You're not crazy, baby, you're just young.

Oh come off it, daddy, I'm thirty. Thirty-one this June. Her voice is rich with disgust.

She is making him remember now the last time she came home. It's not really the money, Adele had to explain, she's afraid to wait much longer, thinks they'll be mongolian idiots or something. He feels his stomach sag, his shoulders droop. Thirty's young, he begs her to believe. She's still trying to shake the railing. Don't do that, he says sharply, it's not meant to take that kind of punishment. Warning her not to wake her mother, he closes the door so carefully there is not the faintest click.

3

Hearing them come up the stairs with a burglar's tread, Adele gently derided their caution. A look at the clock confirmed her suspicion that without her in the car, he was always speeding. She breathed out a gratefulness—Mike back, safe and sound—and as if only then free to acknowledge that she was freezing, drew up the comforter again. How, at this late date, three years into menopause, a hot flush still could take her by surprise—Mike's thermostat had gone crazy, not her body—was beyond her understanding. Except that all her life, her body had surprised her, she had been just as startled by each month's flow.

They were whispering in the hall. Saying goodnight. Get up and say hello, Adele commanded, but shame held her down. She burrowed deeper under cover. Theresa's coming home, Mike announced, and her reaction? Pure rage. Stubbed out now, the way she used to stub out a cigarette when she heard Theresa coming. But that girl had a nose, would smell it on her—just as she had always smelled the faintest aftertrace of tobacco—a rancid odor clinging to her nightgown or her hair, or taste it when they kissed.

That much she owed Theresa—those incessant threats of cancer in both lungs, dead at forty, had worn her down, she *had* stopped smoking. Stopped seeing Evan too, afraid of a more deadly retribution. Mike never noticed anything, it took a child of nine to smell it out. I don't *like* Mr. Novak, Theresa had announced. Adele's heart stopped when Mike asked why. Be-be-cause—back came the stutter of babyhood, Mike looked concerned, Adele thought she would die—be-because he smells. And Mike was so relieved she had finally got it out, he didn't make his usual courtroom objection to prejudicial bias, had merely signaled over her head: what a child!

My child, Adele said out loud, and was startled by the wetness on her cheeks, followed the lazy trickle of two abstract tears. Remembered her father after his stroke. I'm Adele, she said. Adele, he repeated and started to cry. Because he's so glad to see me, she had thought. Because it had no meaning, she knew now.

The door opened on the night-light in the hall, closed again, the darkness now connubial. Mike felt his way to the bed, sat on it gingerly. All the time he was undressing, Adele gave no sign of being awake, telling herself tomorrow would be soon enough. But as soon as his head hit the pillow, she spoke up.

"Did you find out what's wrong?"

Mike took his time, figuring out his move. If he said he didn't think it right to ask, she would say he didn't want to know. "All she would talk about was what they were doing to Union Station."

"All the way from the airport, that was the conversation?"

"Didn't I tell you, she came down by train."

Adele did a push-up in surprise. "That's crazy. A five-hour trip, and then you have to make a change at—" Another thought, of no surprise. "I suppose that's when she called—between stations? Nice of her to let us know."

"She apologized for that. The trouble was she was not sure she was coming at all until she actually got on the train."

Adele could see only a mound of shoulders, the hump of hips, could not locate his head. Of course not, she thought, it's buried in the sand.

"You're a sweet man, Mike," she said and, determined to match his sweetness, merely asked whatever had gotten into the girl, to take a train.

"She's on some kind of nostalgia kick, you know Theresa." The real question was should he even try to get some sleep, it hardly seemed worthwhile. "Funny how kids today like those old movies of the thirties and the forties."

Adele laughed, a short self-deriding bark. Sounds like a seal, Mike thought. "What about us? Wasting a whole evening on *Gone with the Wind?*"

Mike was annoyed, why bring that up? "Forget *Gone with the Wind,* what I'm telling you is Theresa took off as Carole Lombard on a train called the Twentieth Century and she found the snack bar something of a disappointment."

"So's my tapioca pudding—she doesn't say so but I can tell."

Mike noticed she had drawn her knees up, her body in a tight self-protective curl, the way she used to when she had cramps. He gave her behind an affectionate pat. "Relax," he said, "you're always expecting trouble."

At that Adele sat up. Over her bent knees, the covers made a tent open to the cold. "You weren't so relaxed, as I recall, last time she came home. Surrogate mother, remember that one?" A new and more lucrative career, was the way Theresa put it. Nine months of taking it easy, and ten thousand clear. "You don't call that trouble? You sure acted like it was trouble, the way you carried on."

"Crazy," Mike said, his voice robbed of all conviction by sudden overwhelming fatigue. He had managed to make a mummy roll of his share of the covers, was just getting warm. "Talked her out of it though, didn't I? That's why she comes home. Ten thousand for a baby is peanuts, remember Sam, I asked her. A million wasn't enough for him, and he was just a dog."

"I remember Sam." Adele sighed, as if exhaling the memory from her lungs. Poor dog, what Theresa put him through, always testing for devotion. Slam the front door, hide outside, pretend that she was gone (that terrible howl: abandoned! utterly abandoned!) just so she could rush back in and cover him with kisses.

"If someone offered you a million dollars, would you sell Sam? If someone offered you a million dollars, would you sell Sam? If someone offered you a million dollars—" Abruptly Adele dropped the mimicry of a child's insistent pitch. "That one I could answer—after all, you couldn't give a dog like that away. But then she'd come up with the stumper: Suppose we were all in a lifeboat on the ocean, and none of us could swim, and the boat was sinking because there were too many in it, somebody had to get out, would you jump and save us all?" Adele bit her lip. Would I, she was wondering again. "All I could think of to say was don't ask such silly questions. You, on the other hand, passed the test with flying colors. *Daddy* didn't think it silly, *Daddy* said he'd jump out and save us all."

Such resentment. Mike thought it funny. "And so I would, so I would . . . ." But already his laugh was half a snore. He forced himself awake—there was something else besides the train. His eyes closed. Came Theresa in new disguise, still smelling of vanilla. Theresa was a banker now, had forged herself a new degree. He must tell Adele. Did so, and promptly fell asleep.

Easy for him, Adele complained to the black void overhead. Head in sand, doesn't see anything, he can sleep. Drowning was hardly the occasion to review your life, she had always thought; far better, wakefulness at 4:00 A.M. She called them up—the same two questions always conjoined, like Siamese twins sharing a vital organ no surgeon's knife could divide. What if little Michael had not died in his crib, what if big Michael had not survived the war? Tonight they failed her, she could imagine no other life but the one she had led, no fine young man who might have been her son, or whom she might have married in Mike's stead. That old poem was wrong. I don't give a damn were far sadder words than any mere might have been.

She reached out to touch Mike, meaning an apology of sorts. Wrapped in a cocoon, sleeping like a baby. She may not have married a Clark Gable who could work his dimples and break down her door— dear Mike, too good manners for anything like that—but at least she had given birth to Tony Curtis in *The Great Imposter,* that charming, ingratiating, well-meaning liar who obtained an unending procession of highly professional jobs—a surgeon yet!—through false credentials, for which he had no qualifications, unless you count sheer competence as one. Saved in the end, if she remembered rightly, by the love of a good woman. But not in his female incarnation, not Theresa. Not with the men she picked.

Theresa!—she had meant to address her daughter with sweet reason, as she had the child, but the name erupted as a shriek—go away, Theresa, I've stopped bleeding.

As if he had heard her, Mike whimpered, rolled over, broke from cover, arms flailing wildly, a man drowning, cries for help bubbling out of his throat. "It's just a dream, Mike, wake up, you're dreaming." He shuddered at her touch, quieted down. Wifely duty done, Adele got up, shivering even in the flannel robe. Only one blanket on that bunk, she had suddenly remembered, Theresa would be freezing. From the hall closet she took down the feather comforter hand-quilted by her own mother.

The huddled form barely fit within the bunk. Nine months of taking it easy and ten thousand clear, she could hear Theresa explaining. Ten thousand wasn't bad for a few hours' labor. You were right, Adele advised her sleeping daughter. Take the money and run. But still she stayed there a while, not even noticing the cold, marveling anew at how quiet and regular was this child's breathing.

Those Grand Old Songs

On a clear day, Nana could remember forever. She could recite the names of her children in alphabetical order. She knew which was which and who was who and the living from the dead. She was particularly strong on popular songs, words and music, pre-World War I. The Great War, she called it. Grand old songs.

Mothers have favorites, she whispered to her pillow. Like that other secret—oh, those ass's ears!—imparted to the grass, the rumor spread like wildfire.

"You called me Caroline—don't you remember who I am?"

"Of course," Nana said. She knew a hawk from a handsaw. "I just happened to remember a grand old song. It goes like this: *Good evening, Caroline* . . . dum te dum, de dum te dum . . . *never saw you looking finer, how's your ma? how's your pa?* There's no law against singing, is there?"

Two-timing lovers must learn caution (call them all darling in the dark). Daughter, Nana called her now. All of them she called Daughter, when and if they telephoned.

"Here's something new." Daughter was suspicious by nature. "What's the matter? Don't you know our names?"

Nana recited them in alphabetical order. Then why not use them, Daughter pressed. Nana was ready for that. Just tit for tat, she claimed. No one in this house ever called her by *her* name.

"The children called you Nana when they were little. I went along so they wouldn't be confused. It's not the same."

In a face worn down to bedrock, Nana's eyes were beady as a rat's. Bright with cunning. Life was an experiment. She had learned the maze.

"Now Granny," she said, tasting Granny on her tongue, "I like Granny, I wouldn't mind if you called me Granny. Not at all."

"You know that's what they called their other granny—they would really be confused. We would all be confused."

"I know a way to tell us apart." Nana tilted toward her confidentially. "She's dead and I'm not."

Daughter was on the ropes. Nana danced a jig in the middle of the ring; sportsmanlike, held out a hand. "Nana's all right. I don't mind."

Nana watched her descend the stairs, then started for her room, singing, more croak than croon: ". . . *never saw you looking finer . . . how's your pa? how's your ma?*"

Nana found her way in darkness by counting doors. Her hands moved from knob to knob, as if this midnight passage were a mountain-climbing art, a move from piton to piton sunk in the vertical face of rock.

On one side all the doors. On the other the railing over which the children leaped like lemmings. Faster than the stairs. A shortcut, like cutting across the grass. Oh, to leap like that! was Nana's dream.

"Nana will keep an eye on you," Daughter, departing, never failed to warn.

Nana was Argus-eyed. Nana never slept. Nana smoked in bed. Played bridge, all four hands. Dealt them face down on the counterpane, picked each hand up in turn, fanned it out, keeping a poker face. Bid. Smartly laid it down, concealing it from view. Won the contract. Surreptitiously signaled the proper lead. Scraped out a victory with a daring finesse.

The twins flashed by. ("For Chrissake, if you must smoke, keep the door open." Daughter, giving up on lung cancer, now threatened with fire.) Nana heard them storm back up the stairs, returning to the starting gate. Saw them bump each other past her door again, like the uncoordinated halves of a burlesque team impersonating a quadruped.

This time Nana had a better view. Through a hinged crack, a six-foot-long, two-inch-wide slice of life. Oh, to leap like that! The running start, the half-twist of a diver's art! Delight drew her to the railing edge. The sofa below served as trampoline. The two compact cylindrical bodies rose and fell like smoothly functioning pistons illustrating some law of mechanical force.

Nana took back all the nasty things she had said of Daughter's house. (Such as, what's a cathedral ceiling doing in such a nonreligious home? Such as, bedrooms should open on a balcony outdoors, not on a living room eight feet below.) The twins, bless them—bless them, Nana always said of little children, to cancel out the darker wishes that sprang to mind—had justified to her her Daughter's ways.

Even in the darkness the railing drew her. She could sense the sofa there beneath her. Long since resigned to being jumped on, placidly it waited. She could see them leaping, landing, bouncing, stifling screams of joy.

"Nana! What are you doing out here in the dark?"

Nana blinked in the sudden light. An apparition, in see-through nightie. Nana turned her eyes away, tapped her racing heart. Just on her way to tinkle, she explained to Caroline.

"You just called me Caroline."

"You scared the daylights out of me. No wonder."

"It's not the first time."

"Names are my weak spot," Nana confessed, "but I'm good at faces."

"Perhaps you'd rather live with *her*—shall we ask again?"

"She has just three tiny rooms," Nana quoted accurately, "hardly space to turn about."

And Corliss was a Pisces, had worked out Nana's horoscope on a beautiful chart, proving it would never do. Nana had it hanging on her wall, a work of art. Jimmy was a boy, didn't count. Each year Nana sent a card. *So you are*—checked the calendar, checked her Bible, wrote in the allotted space—*sixty-two!* (a fine tremor, barely noticeable, just enough to render *Love, Mother* suspect as a forgery). Marion? Marion was a vexatious thought. Nana pulled a tough hair on her chin as a mnemonic aid, grinned in a triumph of recall. Marion was dead. And so, oddly in order, were Nora and Paul. Ronnie was arthritic, bad-tempered to boot. Tessie had enough on her hands with three Great Danes.

"You are my youngest," Nana said and hoped the snivel would imply the fondness that was youngest's due.

Daughter heaved a sigh and shook her head. Nana had a kaleido-scopic view of the family face, gene-bits resettling. Mother from another time and place. Mother shaking her head too: *Child, you'll be the death of me yet,* with a chest that heaved as deep a sigh though freshly starched and ironed and corset-hard. And so I was, Nana gave Daughter her death's-head grin. And so are we all.

Nana tinkled, went back to her room humming a tune that had been a hit in 1902.

Nana waited impatiently for Daughter's third to assume his rightful place at the head of the table (a temporary position, in Nana's judg-ment; third husbands rarely had tenure). A good carver, Nana gave him that, but his dinner conversation was a bore.

"Nana, tell me, the way you keep shoveling it in, how do you stay so thin? Take my mother. She must have weighed close to three hundred when she died, yet she ate like a bird."

Nana had no patience with a man who believed what his mother told him.

"I burn it up," she said. "I am one of those rare people who never need sleep. Please pass the corn. Was it not Napoleon—" she was being arch, she knew damn well it was Napoleon—"who said seven hours for a man, eight for a woman, and nine for a fool?"

Daughter's third took ten when he could get it. Nana laughed, rattling and spewing kernels in the air like an old farm combine in need of a lube job.

Daughter asked the boy to pick up Nana's napkin from the floor. The boy did, reminding himself, "Do you know that we're built on gar-bage?" Reminding Nana that was the trouble with puberty—the con-stant state of shock at what lies beneath the floorboards. The boy was fourteen. No one entered his room now without a warning knock.

Daughter demanded of her third that he take a look at that sofa after dinner. "I've never seen such inferior workmanship! The springs are shot already, the whole thing's coming apart. Everything's a rip-off nowadays. Nothing lasts!" But that was always Daughter's complaint.

The whole house shrugged with indifference, settling a little deeper in the landfill.

"Garbage!" the boy insisted. "Do you realize what that means? All this was once under water!"

"So were the Appalachians," said Daughter's third, who prided himself on taking the longer view. And as always when disasters were discussed, brought the conversation around to himself. "Talk about workmanship, what about my new car? I'm in cruising speed, right? The car ahead of me slows down for the exit. In the left lane, there's this tractor-trailer. You get the picture? I put my foot on the brake, nothing happens. I'm locked into cruising. I press to the floor. I keep cruising."

Daughter was unimpressed. Even she admitted her third lacked the storyteller's art. "They recall cars. I never heard them recall a sofa. Just look at those cushions when you go in there. You would think a herd of elephants had used them as a ˌstamping ground."

"May we be excused?" the twins politely asked.

"Don't you want to know what happened?" The man looked mortally wounded. Nana was amused. Could he not see the anticlimax of his presence bored them all? Like Old Man River—Nana's head began to bob. She started up with a politic hum, but the finale swept her into open song—"he just keeps cruising, he just keeps cruising, he just keeps cruising along."

Daughter's third flung down his napkin, pushed back his chair. "I'll tell you one thing, she'd better stop that goddam singing. I've had it up to here with what she calls those grand old songs!"

There was nothing wrong with Nana's hearing. She turned on the bedside lamp, propped herself up. "That you, sweetie?"

The boy stuck his head in the door. "You awake, Nana?" He looked younger than she remembered. Tomorrow he would look older than she remembered. A shifty age.

"I never sleep," she said, squinting one-eyed in her smoke. The boy, on the other hand, did nothing but. If home at all. Slept through the parties. Slept through the after-parties, those marital accountings which were sometimes even noisier. Daughter had a ladylike screech, but piercing as a factory-whistle in a one-factory town. Daughter's third boomed out his curses, a cannonade that blasted all upstairs. Getting up to tinkle, Nana knew just where she'd find the twins. On the top step, like rooters in the bleachers, hugging their knees, keeping score. The boy—whenever Nana checked—would still be sleeping, asprawl in the royal position, head under blankets, feet still in dirty gym socks, taking the air.

"Feel like a game of spit?" Nana was being generous. Usually she played the twins, laid off the boy. He could beat her, did without a qualm.

She dealt out the double solitaire with hands trimmed down to bone, functionally spare as a metal prosthesis, the function, grasping.

The boy beat her. "You wanna play *again?*" He knew only disgust for a loser coming back for more.

Nana could tell he had something on his mind. "Just one more," she wheedled, refiguring the odds, narrowing the spread.

The boy shuffled, taking his time. "I sure had a funny dream."

"Mmmm?" Nana encouraged. She had her piles laid out, she was raring to go.

"I was coming home late at night from this basketball game—are you gonna listen?"

Nana said sure, she was listening, he could tell her all about it while they played. They played. More like a tarot reading, it turned out. The boy put down a seven on her eight *(something terrible had happened inside the house)*. She played her jack on his ten before he could reach his nine *(outside, the place was crawling with police)*. Nana slammed down six cards in a row, while the boy's hand hovered over terror, finally dropped a queen.

"—and then this cop comes up and says, this here the weapon, chief? And the chief nods his head, and I look at it and it's my new Louisville Slugger Dave Winfield bat—"

Ah yes, the dream. Nana nodded benignly. The queen was what she needed. Merrily, merrily, merrily life is but a—

"Nobody said so, it just came to me. You had all been killed."

Nana shrugged impatiently, moved up an ace.

"They kept asking funny questions, like where I'd been and who with. I knew what they were getting at."

Salvation by good works, not faith, somebody ought to tell the boy. Damnation by deeds, not by dark intent. Nana opened her mouth to sermonize, saw her opening. She had a glorious run, emptied her hand, cawed with triumph. Pure slaughter!

"—and then I asked myself how come I knew you were all dead inside the house when they hadn't said a word about it. That's when I woke up, and Jesus was I glad I did!"

Forget it, was Nana's advice. "A dream is just a dream." The inevitable refrain popped into her mind. *Just remember this, a kiss is but a kiss . . .* "As time goes by," she finished in a quavering swell. As songs went, not so old perhaps, but it reminded her of Daughter's father—reason enough to include it among the grand.

"Yeah, but Paul, this friend of mine, his brother's taking Freud and Marx this semester, he's always telling Paul what *his* dreams mean, and Paul says—but I dunno. Paul says they both got just one thing on their mind, Freud *and* his brother—"

"That quack," Nana said. "Freud, I mean, not your friend's brother. Marx, now, I haven't made my mind up. The Commies did us Wobblies in, you know. I haven't forgotten that. Not by a long shot."

The boy looked confused. Wobblies? Some kind of senior citizen group?

"Now, sweetie," Nana said, not sweetly, but like a rap on the knuckles, never one to suffer fools. She had tried teaching grade school once, hadn't lasted the term. "I told you before about the IWW—"

"No, you didn't. You told me something—I forget the initials, but it wasn't that. Like the USO, you said."

Nana waved a scrawny arm to discount the discrepancy, dropped a live ash in the bedcovers. The boy raked it out. "That was later, sweetie. Have you no sense of time? Don't you know anything? The Wobblies were *against* the war—the Great War, I hope you know I mean. I split with them on that. But it's true, I did do my bit entertaining the troops." She snickered. "A well-turned ankle, Mr. Belasco said, now show me the rest of the leg. I showed him how well-turned I was. If the war hadn't ended when it did, I might have been a star. Four kids, but still a waist like that, and my hair let down reached below my knees."

"Yeah," the boy said, "but to get back to—"

"The Wobblies, yes," Nana said firmly. "Freedom of speech, that's what we were fighting for, remember that. We stuffed their jails so full, there was no more room, they had to give in. Remember that, sweetie, when something has to give, see that it isn't you. As I recall, that was in ought-eight—no, let me think—" Nana frowned, measuring time not by great floods or prolonged droughts or volcanic eruptions, but by the child in arms, clicking the years on an abacus of little heads—"musta been 1910, I was nursing Corliss, bless her, at the time."

"To get back to the dream," the boy said stubbornly. Stubbornness was his father's side. Nana lost all patience, closed her eyes. "I know what's bugging me. That bat I bought—it's a thirty-six-incher. I was swinging it in my room tonight, the damn thing's too heavy, I'll never get it around fast enough."

He yawned. The dream was safely interpreted and she had won a game—Nana was doubly satisfied. She said no to watching an old movie on TV, demanded a good-night kiss instead.

Whose was this face leaning over her? Boy of a thousand faces—mother, father, uncles, aunts, a perfect stranger (some long-forgotten ancestor?), Nana herself coming to the fore, receding, a struggle for final dominance reflecting an even fiercer inner war.

Suddenly she had to know. "All dead? Even your Nana too?"

The fresh terror of his look told her, Nana too. Bless him, she remembered just in time and sent him on his way and closed her eyes. Not to sleep—Nana never slept—but to count the rhythmic slaps of a jump rope on hard sun-baked ground (white stockings on her legs, ruffles on her petticoat, and an undone gingham sash), winding herself up like a spring with the preliminary rhyme: *Lizzie Borden took an ax, gave her mother forty whacks, when she saw what she had done, she gave her father forty-one.* Then jumping in: ONE, two, three, four, five, six . . . .

Nana could tell from the mess in the kitchen there would be a party. She tried on the kimono Jimmy had sent her, liked the way it looked. The sleeves had an autonomous grace, moving on their own, but the front had a tendency to gape. She needed a pin.

Nana knocked twice before Daughter heard her.

"Oh, is that you, Nana? Come on in."

Daughter stood in the doorway of her private bath—Nana envied that—with the hairdryer pointed like a gun. Not a stitch on. Nana looked away.

"What's the matter, Nana, you didn't use to be so modest."

"I was just wondering if you had a pin."

"Look on the dressing table there. They're in a jar."

Daughter pointed the gun at her head, clicked the trigger and left her on her own. The dressing table was spread like an oriental bazaar with cosmetic jars. With the magnifying glass Daughter used when plucking hairs, Nana read: *Replaces precious lost oils.* A dab of that wouldn't hurt. *Lubricates dry crepey lines.* And a dab of that. *A blend of rich emollients.* And a dab of that.

No jar with pins that she could see. She found it at last on the night table, beside a book left open face down, a sure way to crack the spine. *Joy of Sex?* Nana queried the title and went back for the magnifying glass.

Daughter's third walked in and immediately doubled over with laughter. "It's the magnifying glass, I can't help it! Let me know, Nana, if you find something we have missed. Or something you have missed—that's more like it. All these years, eh? Take it with you, I wish you joy."

In walked the twins, followers of laughter. "What's so funny?" they wanted to know. Nana looked at them, ready for a bath, stripped down to white cotton panties.

"Joy? You call that joy?" She meant to laugh, even as he had laughed, but it came out a short broken-off expulsion of breath, a "hah" of pain. It had hit her in the stomach, what joy was, and yes, God, she missed it! To jump, to run, to climb, to roll, to kick, to leap, to kneel, to hop, to twirl, to bend, to squat, to skip, to dance! Joy? Nana smiled at the twins as frighteningly as when she threatened to eat them up. Joy was to have moveable joints, a backbone flexible as a Slinky toy, and to walk about in white cotton panties with nothing to show above the drum-tight belly but two little nipples, hardly more than moles.

"Thanks, but no thanks." Nana closed the book as a book should be closed, and switched the ferocious grin to him.

Daughter came in, with finished machine-blown hair.

"I've found my pin," Nana said and exited with a cheerful thought—
the two of them in bed together, the book closed, their place lost.

Daughter kept abreast: dressed down for dinner, served wine and
cheese. It was a party. From the balcony, Nana spied on Daughter's
third coming on, feeling up, making out, favoring most—Nana couldn't
believe her eyes but there it was—a woman with a diamond in her nose.

People from the city patronized the view. Nana's foot tapped out
iambs: The boy stood on the burning deck, Garbage! he shouted and
fell down dead.

"You wouldn't want the heating bills, I assure you," Daughter said
with becoming modesty.

Little balloons of conversation floated up. Tennis, squash, handball,
jogging. Life in the city was more strenuous now. And no one smoked.
Nana, on her way to the bathroom, had brought her pack, now pulled it
out. (Must you? Daughter complained, even in the bathroom? I've
never been constipated a day in my life, Nana pointed out.)

Nana smoked. The women asked each other, what do you do? Nana
repeated the names of her children in alphabetical order and flicked her
ashes down. The woman dressed like a piano sent up a shriek, shook
out her fringed paisley shawl.

"Is that you up there, Nana?"

Nana stood on point, took a bow, pantomimed "just on my way to
tinkle," pantomimed "don't mind me," pantomimed "pretend that I'm
not here."

"A remarkable woman, my wife's mother." That was Daughter's
third when he was high, passing compliments with the lavish gestures
of a magician pulling flowers, colored scarfs, cute little bunnies, all
kinds of remarkable surprises out of an ordinary-looking hat. "Don't
ask her age, she won't tell you, but she's ninety if a day." He thought
no doubt that he was speaking low. "Aha, I know what you're thinking." So did Nana. She held a sleeve up, tittered coyly as a geisha.
Daughter's age, that's what they were totting up. "But wait until you
hear her story. Married at sixteen and bam, bam, bam, eight kids, two
husbands down. Then the pause that refreshes, some twenty years. By
then it's mandatory retirement age, you'd think—at least for motherhood. But no, she hitches up with yet another stud, considerably her

junior and quite a looker if you believe the pictures. And whaddya know, it's bam again, one last glorious bam, to which I owe my present happiness." A bow to Daughter, which Nana felt should rightfully be hers. "What say we give the little lady a great big hand?"

They gave a hand. Nana preened. That recounting of her life left out a lot, but what he said was true. Quite a looker—that was true. She had always been a sucker for those warning signs put up by liquor stores just before a dry state line. Last Chance Saloon. Last chance for fun and games, was what she had in mind. Babies, she would have passed right by. I guess I know when I'm not wanted, Daughter never missed a chance to say, ever in a huff, ever walking hoity-toity out of rooms. Not when it counts, you don't, was the retort that always came to Nana's mind.

Beneath the balcony, out of sight, someone sneered in an aside, "But did it last?" Nana considered yelling down, damn tootin' it did, remembered just in time that Daughter was right. Nothing lasts. The looks had held, but the heart gave out.

"Come on down, Nana. Join the party." Daughter's third was high all right. Nana couldn't make her mind up. A buzz of wonder: was it safe for her to use those stairs? Much talk of hip bones broken, aged relatives carried to their final rest. Daughter's eyes glared no! Talons of an eagle grasped the railing. "Don't mind if I do," Nana said, grinning down. What a surprise if like the twins she vaulted over and bounced and bounced and bounced, legs tucked under, arms extended, like a chicken fluttering to roost. She headed toward the stairs, but Daughter moved faster, met her at the top. Hissed, "You can't come down, you're not even dressed."

Nana argued it was a kimono, not a robe. "Jimmy sent it to me. All the way from Japan." Fluttered the arms to show the sleeves that almost touched the floor. Burnt a hole in one, but in that much sleeve, it would never show. Fortunately Daughter was too mad to notice.

Down below, Nana held court. Darling old lady, she was toasted with wine. Tiny little thing, they toasted her again. "Still very much with it, isn't she?" That called for another.

"Three husbands, not bad," said the woman with the diamond in her nose.

Nana knew when she was being patronized. Part of the view. But "thank you, dearie," was all she said.

"Must run in the family." The diamond sparkled when she smiled. The smile was aimed at Daughter's third.

That got Nana's dander up. Damn fool woman, didn't she know the statistics couldn't be compared? Like the boy said, livelier ball, bigger gloves, hollowed-out bats. A different ball game. The rules had changed.

"I buried *my* mistakes." Nana made the point with her cigarette and the woman, vulnerable in gauze, fell back. That was a doctor joke, Nana remembered, and began to laugh.

The hand grasping her elbow was jailor-firm. "Time for beddy-bye," Daughter said.

Nana reminded her that she never slept, but was led inexorably toward the stairs.

"Let's sing some songs!" Nana cried to the crowd. "All you do is stand around and talk. Can't someone here play the piano? How about 'Harvest Moon'? 'Oh, You Beautiful Doll'? 'Wait Till the Sun Shines, Nellie'? 'Love Me and the World is Mine'?"

Daughter tightened her grasp as Nana called down from the balcony, a last desperate try. "Here's a good one—'Waltz Me Around Again, Willie.' Anybody remember how it goes?"

She might be a little unsteady on her feet, but she remembered how it went.

". . . around, around, around, the music is dreamy, it's peaches-and-creamy, oh, don't let my feet touch the ground!"

She was still singing when Daughter firmly closed her door.

Little Boy Blue

From the elevator emerged a large woman in a voluminous cape. A lighter-than-air craft, tethered to earth by the fragile underpinning of thin ankles and narrow bony feet. A dirigible of a body, billowing and bouncing, emitting even in the breezeless lobby fine streamers of fly-away hair. The large round expanse of face was like a face painted on a balloon—the always present smile gave her features just that kind of spread. Mrs. Phillips was fifty-five, but gave no sign that age would ever deflate her. Her skin was tight, her step elastic. To look into her eyes could still be dizzying, a sudden ascent into the blue.

Instinct raised her arms against the wobbling pigskin projectile. Ah, that smile. Even Al the doorman, dour tenant-hater, eternal taker of civil service exams, smiled back as she intercepted the pass. Skidding to a halt on the marble lobby floor, the boy almost knocked her down. Mrs. Phillips kept her balance only by clawing at the thin lettered jersey, delighted—the smile insisted—to find a football nestled against her breast.

"How many times I told that kid, *not* in the lobby!" Simulated outrage, Al knew she knew. She had seen him fading back to make the catch himself. "See what you done, Martin. What if Mrs. Phillips had fallen, broke a leg. A nice lady like her." Any other tenant would have been fair game, the implication was there.

"Not *Martin?*" The super's oldest in her grasp, who surely, only yesterday—Mrs. Phillips questioned her memory—had been of head-patting height? Yet here they stood, shoulder to shoulder, eye to eye. The boy apologized. She felt undone by that cracked voice of youth. At such close range, the childish smudge of dirt above his upper lip turned out to be the first silky growth of hair.

He had to ask for the ball. She was still holding it as if in forfeit. First she must be told why he was not in school, a weekday morning like this.

"Bomb threat." A bored yawn of an announcement, with a sideward glance to see the effect.

She shuddered satisfactorily. "How terrible! A school!"

"Third time this month." The boy shrugged. "They never find nothing."

Terrible, she repeated the shudder, causing Al to mock her with a "terrible" of his own. Funny, he addressed the high coffered ceiling, bomb threats always arrived on days like this—perfect football weather. "Ain't you better get a move on, Martin? You must be holding up the game."

Mrs. Phillips tossed the ball back. She hoped out loud that their Martin was not involved in tricks like that. Her blue eyes darkened receptively as she viewed his jerky embarrassed exit through the revolving door. She remembered him as a thin and stringy boy. His shoulder blades still pierced that jersey like incipient wings, but certain changes were taking place. A lumpiness around the hips, an almost feminine waddle as the buttocks moved, some transient storage of fat to nourish the furious spurt of growth. Three inches in as many months, she estimated. And within, withal, what hormonal storms.

"That age, that age." The headshake was reproving, but there was sweet-breathed nostalgia in the sigh. "They're either outdoors playing to the death or indoors sleeping for hours on end." Her eyes crinkled in reminiscence, in which her smile invited Al to join.

He had a foreboding. He could see it coming. This conversation, he tried to make her understand, was at an end. Out came his pipe, at which he knew most tenants took offense. (At that and at his full moustache; surely doormen and baseball players should be subserviently clean-shaven.) He took his accustomed seat in a Tudor chair facing the door, restoked the bowl, lit match after match, sucked loudly, and stared everywhere but at Mrs. Phillips herself. Thus he cut tenants short in mid-complaint.

But Mrs. Phillips's smile was not so easily dismissed. "I'm sure he would be glad to have some of Jonathan's things—"

There it was. That name. Al signaled his confusion in furious puffs.

"—I don't mean old clothes, but football helmets are expensive, as I recall, and Jonathan's must still be lying about somewhere. Just the other day I ran across a football, not a scuff on it, good as new. Send the boy up some afternoon, Al, he might want to take a look."

Al grunted, made a noise with his pipe that said he would, that said he wanted to hear no more about a Jonathan who had it made—nice home, nice parents, nice school—and threw it all away. Jumped from a penthouse window his first Christmas home from Yale. Al glared unforgivingly through the revolving door at the spot where a covering tarp once lay. He didn't remember the football gear. The picture he had was of racer shorts, tennis racket, matchstick legs—the boy as tall as his father, and the two of them, like sparring partners, clean white towels draped around their necks, jogging off to the courts. Mr. Phillips now (she never mentioned *him*), there was a father who really enjoyed his son. Kept in good shape and proud of it; thumped his flat stomach, poked Al's soft middle, went out to play in the hottest weather, when even the boy looked beat.

Never a neglected kid—Al's doorman memory went back to sandbox days to vouch for that. The little boy walked beside his mother, holding his pail and shovel with the aplomb of an old-fashioned gentleman holding a hat and cane. Some snappy dresser, Al had teased him. Even his T-shirts were pressed. And never a hand laid on him, not even in the tantrum stage. There, where this morning's sun had unrolled a runner of light, a stuffed-toy form in zippered snowsuit once lay, asprawl on cold marble, screaming bloody murder. *I'd spank him if that was my child.* That was the old lady in 6-A (where the two queers now lived), always loitering in the lobby for her mail. Mrs. Phillips never touched him. All the time in the world was the impression she gave. Al could still see her standing there, holding the elevator open, waiting for the screams to stop. The patience of a saint. Never lost her smile. Al had been in awe of her for that. Was awestruck now, to hear her name him with the same undiminished smile. As if he had left home, like other kids this building had spawned, in the ordinary way.

Mrs. Phillips gave him a complicitous wink. "Football weather," she said and laughed as she adjusted her cape, prepared to meet the wind. He watched her move through the revolving door with no apparent effort, as if the floor on which she stood did all the turning. The cape blew out behind her. There was something of the schoolgirl in her awkward grab for the hood, the way she hitched the leather portfolio under her arm. On most people, tragedy took its toll. Al had been doorman twenty years. So far as he could tell, she hadn't changed a bit.

"You haven't changed a bit." Two Bloody Marys before lunch lent a certain aggressiveness to her friend's complaint.

The aggressiveness did not take Lorelie by surprise—that was just Ella—but the envy was new. She could not truthfully reply that Ella, once merely dark-eyed, dark-haired pretty, had not changed. Ella was top management now, sexy with success. From the terraced hair to the pointed boots, more admirable in design than any industrial product Lorelie could take credit for. She tried to express in one long fluty breath that, in Ella's case, the change was for the better.

"That's pure shit," Ella said, stopping her cold. "If only I could see you making an effort, straining a little more each year along with the rest of us, it would be easier to take. Hell, you don't even watch your weight. You never did. And it isn't surgery—I checked you for the scars when I helped you off with that silly cape."

Cold hands on her neck, Lorelie recalled.

"What's wrong with the cape?" A matter of tactics. Let Ella use her cutting tongue on that.

"You should see yourself from the back, with no arms. It's something a shoplifter would wear, with hundreds of pockets inside to conceal the loot."

Lorelie tried to look distressed. "I wish you hadn't said that. Now I shall always be looking for those hidden mirrors."

Ella laughed, but was only briefly appeased. She was the one facing the mirror that lined the wall behind the banquette. She was the one who had to watch herself eat.

"The dentist tells me he has to reconstruct my whole mouth or all my teeth will fall out. Do you have any idea of what that involves?"

"It happens to us all," Lorelie said, and carefully blotted her lips with her napkin. Even so, Ella suspected a smile. You would think, Ella thought, a woman whose son had killed himself and whose husband left her not long after would not smile so much.

The waiter presented the dessert menu. Lorelie read it carefully, and Ella, unseeing, gripped it too.

"Look at my knuckles," she cried, "how swollen. I had to have my wedding ring sawed off. There's nothing they can do for arthritis, it can only get worse."

Lorelie's round face was punctured with a sympathetic "oh." She searched for some ache, some twinge of pain, some sign of impending infirmity she might add to the pot. Embarrassed at her failure, she reached down for the portfolio resting against her shins. "You said you wanted to see the new coffee maker I designed—"

"Don't change the subject!" Ella exploded. "That's what I can't stand about you! You always act embarrassed when I mention growing old. As if it were unnecessary. Sheer weakness of character. Damn it, Lorelie, we're the same age; if you don't feel it you must be taking something! What is it?"

Lorelie was still protesting, Ella still unconvinced, when the bill arrived. They dueled for a moment with credit cards. With one flash of her lipstick, Ella had recolored her mouth while Lorelie was still trying to read the time in her tiny old-fashioned gold watch.

"Quarter past," Ella told her. "Late for an appointment? I can drop you off."

"Thank you, dear, but it's hardly necessary. My doctor's office is just around the corner."

"Anything wrong?" There was a perceptible brightening of Ella's mood.

"Just a routine checkup," Lorelie said. Her smile turned down in self-deprecation, then up again for a fond good-bye.

Feet in stirrups, legs apart, she examined the ceiling, searching for the faintest flaw, the first sign of a crack. Each year she forced herself to face this dread moment of truth. Each year a different office, a different doctor, like a criminal covering her tracks. Having opened herself up for judgment, she could never come back.

She felt the condom-slick finger, the speculum's cold bite. How much was revealed? Crumbling dilapidated walls. Room womb only once occupied, yet swept out monthly all those years in case a new tenant should doubtfully knock at the door. Inquire within. And now no more. The last sign taken down, abandoned, gutted. Poor Miss Havisham still sitting there as on her bridal night. Brave man, to even look through the peephole. Behind the fibrous cobwebs, what vile scampering might not be heard, what fetid breath encountered, what maleficent hunchbacked form emerge from the shadows, proclaiming squatter's rights?

"That's fine." The head with the grey comb-raked hair was removed from between her thighs. "Please come into the office when you've dressed."

She would rather not. She would rather have her fortune out of a cookie or a gum machine. She found it difficult to put her clothes back on, nothing hung right. She left the cubicle, feeling slightly askew, like a gift package inspected and then, still to be presented, rewrapped.

In the chair beside the desk she read the walls. Diplomate. Good hospital connections. He entered, obviously a man who had just washed his hands. Sat down and wrote. *Well-nourished Caucasian female.* She could read upside down as well as right side up. Also mirror writing. Spell backwards. Even talk backwards, like a rewinding tape. She had broken every one of Jonathan's cryptic codes. Cries for help. Fun and games, she had thought.

Age?

She gave him not quite the sum total of her years, but close enough. He looked up, surprised. She wondered if she had taken off too much.

Younger, I would have thought.

Do not fall for that, the warning flashed. He may be trying a flank attack. She braced herself in the chair, strapped herself in, as if she had just heard the sweet voice of a stewardess downplaying a little turbulence ahead.

Married, I see.

He saw. Through the eye of the speculum, all was seen. Her thumb folded in, rubbed against the embedded gold band, exposed him as a fraud. Her mother's wedding ring, not hers. Hers lay somewhere in a box along with odd buttons from discarded clothes. Junk jewelry. Alan never did have taste. He left a note, he couldn't say it to her face. This was the only kind of valid wedding ring—wide and heavy and untransmutable. Returned by the funeral parlor in a sealed brown envelope, like valuables checked in with a hotel desk clerk. The dental plate. The tiny watch with its indecipherable face. Burn the rest, she had said dryeyed. But at the funeral she had suddenly let out a shriek—didn't know where the noise was coming from until Charlie patted her on the back as if to dislodge a bolus of unchewed food stuck in her throat. What a surprise, dear long lost brother, had been her greeting to him. For Jonathan, a wire had sufficed. He kept looking around the chapel—she finally realized why. Where was Alan, he was wondering but didn't want to ask. She made him ask. Where's Alan, he asked. Seems, where he was, he never got her letter about the divorce.

Divorced, she corrected the scribbling antiseptic hand.

Any children?

Just the two of us now, Charlie, I said. We'll have to stick closer, Charlie said. Baby brother. How he hated to be called that. Baby. My baby. Girls of nine feel that way when a baby's born. A beautiful baby, a true blond, not a dirty blond like me. I was the one who taught him how to walk. Mother squatted down, held out her arms. I squatted down beside her, held out mine. Whose itsy-bitsy baby are you? Then he shows up for her funeral—twenty years I hadn't seen him—looking like a tramp. Layers of dirty underwear showing at the open neck of his shirt. Between flights, he said. I gave him one of Jonathan's ties. He didn't like the idea, but I made him wear it, to show respect. For your mother, you show respect. You could have written, I said, all these years. I refuse to count Christmas cards. Or condolences when wired, the words counted, for a nephew never seen. Between jobs, he said. Between wives. Between countries. Between lives. Besides, he said, spitting the sarcasm out like a pip, I never knew you cared. I just looked at him. It was the first time, I swear, I saw the resemblance. But Jonathan was handsomer. Much handsomer.

Jonathan, she said, my son.

Age?

A beautiful baby, mother said, takes after our side, remember Charlie at that age? Yes, I told her, I remember Charlie.

Age?

Nine years younger, baby brother, you'd never know it, I'm the one
who's taken care. Did you hear that—he thought I didn't care. Because
I didn't touch. Oh Charlie dear, mustn't touch—we learned that at
mother's knee. And yet—do you remember? no, you were too young,
you could not possibly remember, who remembers the first step taken?
only I remember—you toddled right past mother, came to me. You
came to *me*. And there you are, fixed forever within the circle of these
arms. I didn't tell him that, of course. We're not a demonstrative family, I said, that's the way mother brought us up. And I let him go. As I
let Jonathan go. And Jonathan went and. Not even a note. He should
have left a note, his father did. That nice policeman, the younger one,
taking it so hard, hating to ask those questions. I told him of course I
understood, he had to ask those questions in such cases, I didn't envy
him his job. I knew what he wanted me to say, he wouldn't leave until
he made me say it. I never touched him. You hear that, mother? I never
touched him.

Your son's age? A polite cough. Like the mild tap of a gavel calling
the courtroom to order.

Twenty-two, she said, and waited for the prosecutor to stand up and
shout: will the judge instruct the witness to answer, twenty-two alive or
twenty-two dead?

"Everything's normal, Mrs. Phillips. I recommend a breast exam in
six months, but that's routine. I'm giving you a clean bill of health."

Mrs. Phillips tapped on the bulletproof glass. Once she would have
had the driver wait while she picked up a few forgotten items at the
corner grocery, but today she preferred to walk the remaining two
blocks home. Cab rides had become a claustrophobic experience. She
would have liked to share her euphoria—how competent, in retrospect,
that doctor; how helpful the clerks in the sporting goods store—but it
was impossible to chat pleasantly through a metal grid. She fed the fare
into the trough, concluded the transaction with no contaminating touch
of hands, and extricated herself by stages. First the thin legs, last the
two bulky but lightweight boxes.

The sign was still in the window. *Delivery boy wanted, part-time,
after school.* The ringing bell warned passers-by that the metal trap-

door in the sidewalk was open, exposing the blackness of the nether regions of the store. She picked her way through the barricade of newly delivered cartons. Nine Lives, Nine Lives, Nine Lives, she read.

The owner himself was at the checkout. Outside, on the elevator platform, his lone assistant rose slowly into view. First J. J.'s grizzled head, then his butcher-aproned torso. Such had been her first sight of David. A stagy production, she had thought at the time—enter Mephistopheles, straight up from hell—until she saw how young he was, grinning from ear to ear, enjoying the ride.

"So many cats for customers, Mr. Cracow?" She nodded at the cartons blocking the entrance.

The teasing glint in her blue eyes, the friendliness of her smile, straightened the grocer out of his slouch. If all his customers were like her, he reasoned obscurely, he would have no varicose veins, would not suffer so from piles.

"So many old ladies, Mrs. Phillips." His wink joined them both in the freemasonry of youth.

"It seems so little, I hate to ask for delivery, but—" She held up the boxed trophies of her shopping to explain such an unreasonable request. No trouble, no trouble at all, he was quick to reassure her, though the deadline for delivery had passed. For Mrs. Phillips, J. J. would be glad to make an extra trip.

"I see you have yet to replace David. Such a nice boy. I was so sorry to see him go."

David, she said. Good riddance! he thought, as automatic a response as gesundheit to a sneeze.

"The family moved out of the neighborhood—the kid's got another job closer to his school." He passed the information on, nodding benignly, as if he shared her regret for that goof-off, that no-goodnik, who could take a whole afternoon to make a couple of deliveries just a block or two away.

Mrs. Phillips clucked her sympathy for his loss.

"They come, they go," the grocer said, pleased to show he could meet adversity with a stoic's grace.

Mrs. Phillips sighed. "Yes, they do." Then brightened. She was sure in time he would find another nice young boy.

A problem, his shrug confessed. He spread his hands to show he had no solution as yet. "Can't just take any hoodlum off the street. A lot of these old ladies, they're afraid to open their doors."

They shared another smile at old ladies, and watching J. J. trundle in a heavy load, she offered a considerate suggestion. Until a younger pair of legs was found, J. J. should leave her order with the doorman in the lobby. She was thinking of the last flight of stairs to be climbed after the elevator made its final stop. "The penthouse, you know, is a long way up."

The grocer was struck by the delicate quivering sweetness that bloomed in her face. How like her—to think of J. J.'s age. In the mirror tilted for shoplifters he saw his own face, poxed with meanness, grubby of soul. He stepped to the doorway, saw her turn the corner, her cape billowing as it caught the wind. The two large boxes seemed essential ballast to keep her from being swept away.

For Mrs. Phillips, Al marked his place in the sample civil-service test, got out of his chair, summoned the elevator, pushed the top button.

"Oh, I forgot," he said, catching the door just before it closed on her thank-you smile. "Martin says if it's all right with you, he'll pick up the stuff this afternoon. I'm to let him know when you come in."

She was still breathless from the wind, her fine hair flying apart with an electric charge. The blueness of her eyes was startling, calling into question the claim to blueness of any other eyes Al had ever seen.

"My goodness, so soon." She flung back her cape, tried to read her watch, dropped a box, picked it up before Al could perform his intended gallantry, laughed at their bumping heads. "Give me half an hour, Al. That will be fine."

She took the final flight of stairs lightly as a girl. A tremor of excitement caused a little trouble with the key, but once inside she went directly to Jonathan's room, unwrapped her new purchases. There on the floor of the closet, she placed the shining helmet but the football she held at arm's length, laces forward, taking a moment to admire the design. It seemed more of nature's provenance than man's, as perfect as the egg. She gave it a little envious toss and it wobbled, unscuffed as promised, into a corner.

Out of closet darkness, the memory sprang at her. *The little toy dog is covered with dust* . . . de dum de dum de dum . . . *And the little toy soldier is red with rust* . . . de dum de dum de dum. Eugene Field. Lines learned by heart more than forty years ago were still there, on some forgotten shelf of mind . . . red with rust . . . covered with dust. "Little Boy Blue," oh yes, that was the poem. She had hardly understood the boy's vague demise. It was for the toys she had wept—oh, those sad, dusty, rusty toys. *And they wonder, as waiting those long years through / In the dust of that little chair / What has become of our Little Boy Blue / Since he kissed them and put them there.* The tears too came by rote—unsalted, soft-as-rainwater prepubertal tears. What would children today make of such sentimental rubbish? Martin, say. The thought of Martin returned to her her smile.

Her movements as she undressed were unhurried but efficient, following a routine of folding neatly, hanging up, never glancing at that cornucopia of a body, so slender in the stem, spilling all its bounty at the top. The nakedness moved in and out of mirrors, readying itself.

The doorbell chimed at the same moment that the telephone began to ring. In the bulky toweling of a terry robe (not Venus rising from the sea, but mother fresh from the bath) she opened for Martin and smiled him in, then with an apologetic gesture picked up the foyer phone. Ah, Ella, she said, and asked her to hold on.

Martin was standing just inside the door, shrinking from the white walls, keeping off the Kerman rug, looking as if one step forward and he would break something. Phone to breast, Mrs. Phillips smiled encouragement. "This will just take a moment, Martin. Go right on down the hall to the bedroom at the very end. I'm sure we'll find something for you in there—wait for me and we'll take a look together."

She watched him, already more at ease, saunter down the passageway. How to relieve a young boy's embarrassment? Give him simple directions to follow. An exciting thought. Quickly she unmuffled the phone (had Ella picked up her heartbeat?). "Not at all," she denied, but allowing the tone of her voice to admit the inconvenience of the call. "How sweet of you to worry . . . no, no, nothing like that, you should know I wouldn't keep anything serious from you. Just my yearly

checkup, honest. Everything's normal, I have it on the best authority . . . Yes, thank you, dear. I'm glad you called."

She walked down the hall as one not relying on sight but following a
spoor, and her smile was equally blind, left over from some long-ago
occasion. The roughness of terry massaged her. She tingled with well-
being. Her breasts hung heavy, full of a richness beyond that of milk.
She entered the room where the boy awaited her touch, confident that
he could not escape her. She had had the windows barred.

ILLINOIS SHORT FICTION

Crossings by Stephen Minot
A Season for Unnatural Causes by Philip F. O'Connor
Curving Road by John Stewart
Such Waltzing Was Not Easy by Gordon Weaver

Rolling All the Time by James Ballard
Love in the Winter by Daniel Curley
To Byzantium by Andrew Fetler
Small Moments by Nancy Huddleston Packer

One More River by Lester Goldberg
The Tennis Player by Kent Nelson
A Horse of Another Color by Carolyn Osborn
The Pleasures of Manhood by Robley Wilson, Jr.

The New World by Russell Banks
The Actes and Monuments by John William Corrington
Virginia Reels by William Hoffman
Up Where I Used to Live by Max Schott

The Return of Service by Jonathan Baumbach
On the Edge of the Desert by Gladys Swan
Surviving Adverse Seasons by Barry Targan
The Gasoline Wars by Jean Thompson

Desirable Aliens by John Bovey
Naming Things by H. E. Francis
Transports and Disgraces by Robert Henson
The Calling by Mary Gray Hughes

Into the Wind by Robert Henderson
Breaking and Entering by Peter Makuck
The Four Corners of the House by Abraham Rothberg
Ladies Who Knit for a Living by Anthony E. Stockanes

Pastorale by Susan Engberg
Home Fires by David Long
The Canyons of Grace by Levi Peterson
Babaru by B. Wongar

Bodies of the Rich by John J. Clayton
Music Lesson by Martha Lacy Hall
Fetching the Dead by Scott R. Sanders
Some of the Things I Did Not Do by Janet Beeler Shaw

Honeymoon by Merrill Joan Gerber
Tentacles of Unreason by Joan Givner
The Christmas Wife by Helen Norris
Getting to Know the Weather by Pamela Painter

Birds Landing by Ernest Finney
Serious Trouble by Paul Friedman
Tigers in the Wood by Rebecca Kavaler
The Greek Generals Talk by Phillip Parotti